Getting the Drop on the Gunsmith

The pistol flashed in Clint's eyes like a mirror catching a ray of sun. Even though it hadn't been anything but a flicker of firelight glinting off metal, the sight was enough to put all of Clint's reflexes on the alert.

Clint's hand was a blur of motion as it flashed to his side and wrapped around the handle of the modified Colt waiting for him inside its holster. Without taking his eyes from the gun being held by a man dressed in shabby denim and a dusty hat pushed low over his brow, Clint drew the Colt and brought it up. Although he was supremely confident in his own speed, he wasn't stupid enough to assume he could beat a man who'd already drawn.

Sure enough, as if to prove his fears correct, the man with the gun stepped off slightly to the side and squeezed his trigger. The pistol in his hand let out a thunderous blast and sprayed a shower of sparks into the smoky air . . .

DON'T MISS THESE
ALL-ACTION WESTERN SERIES
FROM THE BERKLEY PUBLISHING GROUP

THE GUNSMITH by J. R. Roberts
Clint Adams was a legend among lawmen, outlaws, and ladies. They called him . . . the Gunsmith.

LONGARM by Tabor Evans
The popular long-running series about Deputy U.S. Marshal Long—his life, his loves, his fight for justice.

SLOCUM by Jake Logan
Today's longest-running action Western. John Slocum rides a deadly trail of hot blood and cold steel.

BUSHWHACKERS by B. J. Lanagan
An action-packed series by the creators of Longarm! The rousing adventures of the most brutal gang of cutthroats ever assembled—Quantrill's Raiders.

DIAMONDBACK by Guy Brewer
Dex Yancey is Diamondback, a Southern gentleman turned con man when his brother cheats him out of the family fortune. Ladies love him. Gamblers hate him. But nobody pulls one over on Dex . . .

WILDGUN by Jack Hanson
Will Barlow's continuing search for his daughter, kidnapped by the Blackfeet Indians who slaughtered the rest of his family.

THE GUNSMITH

245

GHOST SQUADRON

J. R. ROBERTS

JOVE BOOKS, NEW YORK

This is a work of fiction. Names, characters, places, and incidents either are the product of the author's imagination or are used fictitiously, and any resemblance to actual persons, living or dead, business establishments, events, or locales is entirely coincidental.

GHOST SQUADRON

A Jove Book / published by arrangement with
the author

PRINTING HISTORY
Jove edition / May 2002

Visit our website at
www.penguinputnam.com

ISBN: 0-515-13297-7

A JOVE BOOK®
Jove Books are published by The Berkley Publishing Group,
a division of Penguin Putnam Inc.,
375 Hudson Street, New York, New York 10014.
JOVE and the "J" design
are trademarks belonging to Penguin Putnam Inc.

PRINTED IN THE UNITED STATES OF AMERICA

10 9 8 7 6 5 4 3 2 1

ONE

For a soldier, war was always on the horizon.

Peace was nothing more than a prolonged rest between conflicts when armies were fattened, weapons gathered, and funds collected in the pockets of eager governments. Even though most of the high-ranking officers still had the bitter taste of gunpowder in the backs of their throats left over from the War Between the States, that didn't mean that they weren't ready for the next time shots were fired.

If history had taught anything to anyone, it was that there would always be a next time.

For a soldier, that next time was the next war. And to General Anton Waverly, that particular next time seemed closer than it had been for quite a few years.

Still clutching the telegram in his hand, General Waverly read over the words that had been hastily smeared across yellowed paper for what must have been the fifth time in as many minutes. Although as a soldier he was always prepared for war, he wasn't as eager to see the battlefield as the younger men filling up the lower ranks. In fact, he imagined that the telegram he'd just received would have brought a smile to some of those ruddy faces.

Some of the younger troops had yet to fire their rifles

outside of practice drills and were itching for the chance to pull their triggers while the rattle of drums echoed through their ears. But Waverly had seen too many mauled bodies and too much blood to still have such feelings. For him, fighting was his duty. It was his life. There was no more pleasure to be taken from it.

Just to be sure that he wasn't jumping to conclusions, the general leaned forward in his chair and laid the telegram on top of his finely polished desk. Spreading it out like a field map, he placed his hands on either side of the paper, took a deep breath, and scanned the words one more time.

VARILLO'S FORCES CONFIRMED
SOUTH OF TEXAS BORDER **STOP**
INTELLIGENCE REPORTS MAJOR OFFENSIVE EXPECTED
STOP
PRESIDENT REQUESTS DEPLOYMENT
OF GHOST SQUADRON TO AREA
IMMEDIATELY **STOP**
ENGAGE ENEMY ON SIGHT **STOP**

It wasn't the Ghost Squadron that made General Waverly feel uncomfortable. On the contrary, he was the one most responsible for forming the group of elite shock troops assigned to the War Department. The squadron was one of his proudest achievements while serving in the United States Army and he considered every one of those men to be like his son.

What caused the general to shift in his seat and rub his eyes was the thought of that last line in the telegram. ENGAGE ENEMY ON SIGHT.

For the president to issue a command like that meant he was fully expecting a fight. More than that, he wanted to be sure that, once that fight inevitably started, it would be his men to draw first blood.

ENGAGE ENEMY ON SIGHT **STOP**

The words echoed through Waverly's mind as though they'd been spoken directly into his ear. He knew every one of the members of Ghost Squadron personally, just as he knew they were one of the most deadliest fighting forces ever assembled. Once they engaged the enemy, there would be no stopping them.

Not until every member of one side was dead.

That was what worried General Waverly. After working tirelessly for weeks to work out a settlement with Diego Varillo, things were just starting to come together. And now, this happened. Troops were being deployed with the sole intention of wiping Varillo's platoon off the face of the earth.

General Waverly was not accustomed to questioning his orders. Although there wasn't a single piece of his brain that thought ill of his superiors, there was plenty going on inside of him that made him suspicious of this entire situation.

The talks with Varillo had been going so well.

The president had been more than satisfied with the progress that had been made.

And the other higher-ups inside the War Department didn't seem too concerned with Varillo as a genuine threat to the United States, which made a move this drastic sit like a chip of bone wedged in the back of his throat. No matter how hard Waverly tried, he simply could not swallow it.

Finally, the general came to a decision.

Slowly, he raised his eyes from the telegram and removed the reading glasses from his face. As prepared as he was for war, he simply could not allow himself to do something that might start a conflict that would needlessly snuff out so many lives. If this military action went wrong, it could potentially escalate into something truly tragic.

No matter how many times he looked at it, no matter

how many different angles he took, General Waverly couldn't see this order resulting in anything but disaster. Knowing full well how others might view what he was going to do, Waverly pushed his chair away from his desk and stood up so he could turn and look out his window.

After taking in a few moments of serenity while looking out over the well-kept grounds, Waverly turned away from his view of Washington, D.C., and strode to the only door leading out of his office. He opened it just enough to get a look at the smaller desk situated in the next room. Sitting there was a well-dressed man in his early thirties who was hunched over a stack of papers. Setting aside what he was doing the minute he saw the main door open, the younger man looked up at General Waverly.

"Yes, sir?" the young man asked expectantly.

"I need you to come into my office, Bert," Waverly said. "Bring the files on Varillo and his associates. Also, I need to contact Jim West."

Bert's eyebrows raised as he flinched involuntarily. "Jim West? Is there something wrong?"

"There's *going* to be something wrong, I'm afraid. More wrong than I think anyone else could possibly realize."

TWO

At four in the afternoon, Rick's Place was as close to deserted as a saloon its size could ever be. Normally, the bar was fairly well stocked with a good mixture of travelers passing through Labyrinth, Texas, on their way to wherever they might be going, and locals who'd lived in West Texas for most of their lives. Taking up a good portion of the remaining space inside the saloon were tables used for everything from dining to poker, faro, and blackjack.

Rick Hartman had been running his saloon long enough to know when folks would be drifting in or out. The customers came through his place like a constant tide, ebbing and flowing at certain times of day reliably enough for him to set his watch by them. And though one of his best patrons had only recently come back to Labyrinth after nearly a year's absence, the bartender picked up on that one's pattern soon enough. It wasn't too difficult. After all, he'd known the other man for more years than he could remember.

Letting a couple of minutes pass, Hartman pulled a mug from beneath the bar, filled it with a cold beer, and set it on top of the polished wooden corner at the far end. He didn't even bother turning around when he heard the front door swing open and footsteps knock against the floor, approaching his spot.

Clint Adams walked to the end of the bar, looked down at the beer waiting there for him, and shook his head. "Am I really that predictable, Rick?" he asked.

Hartman suppressed a laugh and nudged the mug forward. "Perhaps you'd prefer the phrase 'set in your ways'?"

Doing his best to come up with a way to prove his good friend wrong, Clint tried to ignore the mug while scanning the bottles lined up on a set of shelves behind the bar. Finally, he shrugged and took a sip of the beer. "Okay, so I'm predictable. There's plenty worse things a man can be."

"There sure are. Like a freeloader, for instance. Were you ever planning on paying up the tab you've been running ever since you've gotten back into town?"

Clint paused with the mug still pressed against his lips. For a second, he eyed Hartman over the dented metal rim before setting the mug down and wiping some stray foam from beneath his nose. "Tab? You want to talk about a tab? How about I charge you for all the times you rope me into acting as a bouncer when you get some cowboys in here that want to shoot up the place? Or what about all the cardsharps I roust from your tables? Maybe I'll charge . . . let's see . . . a dollar a head for them. Plus another twenty percent of the cash I take from their pockets that they would've swindled right out from under that crooked nose of yours."

Raising his hands as though he was on the wrong end of a gun, Hartman laughed hard enough to start his belly shaking. "All right, all right," he groaned. "You got me. Drink your damn beer and shut up for a change. Some of us have work to do."

Clint took another sip and let the cool brew wash down

his throat. The bickering between himself and Hartman was more like the harmless fighting between brothers. It always brought a smile to both men's faces and was every bit a vital part of their routine as the beer Clint drank every day at four o'clock.

Even though Clint had only been back in Labyrinth for just over three weeks, he'd quickly settled into a warm state of comfort triggered by allowing himself to stay in such familiar surroundings. Taking up a room at the Lone Star Hotel, Clint was glad to trade in life on the trail for a while . . . no matter how temporary that trade might be.

"So what's the good word?" Hartman asked as he turned his attention from one of the few other customers standing at the bar.

"The good word is that there is no word," Clint replied happily. "At least not for me, anyway."

Refilling drinks for the few other customers who were in his saloon at this time of day, Hartman let out another stifled laugh. When he spoke, his voice was tainted with sarcasm. "Yeah. The quiet life. That's what you're all about, isn't it?"

"Well, I might just be getting used to it. At least, for the time being anyway."

Just then, the saloon's front door swung open to allow a slender man to poke his head inside. He wore a clean white shirt with the sleeves rolled up tightly to his elbows. His balding head was mostly covered by a dented visor and there was a pencil stuck behind his left ear.

Despite the fact that the man looked to be in his late forties, he stepped inside the saloon as though he was committing a cardinal sin. His eyes darted back and forth a few times before settling on Clint like a mouse eyeing a piece of cheese. "Mister Adams?" he asked in a tense, somewhat squeaky voice.

Clint had been watching the man with no small amount of amusement. He recognized the skinny fellow as the man who worked at the telegraph office and greeted him with a wave of his hand. "Over here, Zack. Come on in."

For a moment, Zack seemed reluctant to step inside. But once he set foot into Rick's Place, he scuttled toward the back of the room in quick, short steps. "This just came for you," he said while holding out a folded piece of paper in a pale, bony hand. "Fresh off the wire."

Hartman quickly finished up what he was doing and drifted back to Clint's end of the bar. "A telegram, huh? Who's it from?"

Eyeing Hartman with open disfavor, Zack pulled his hand back just a bit. "It's for Mister Adams. I'm not permitted to tell anyone else what—"

"It's all right," Clint said as he snatched the paper from the mousy clerk. "I'm sure whatever this is, it's no federal matter." By the time he read over the first couple of lines written by Zack's scribbling pencil, Clint felt his stomach tighten into a small knot. "Then again," he grumbled, "I could be mistaken about that last part."

THREE

"What's the matter?" Hartman asked once he saw the humor drain away from Clint's features. "What the hell's that telegram about anyway?"

Clint looked up from the message. Even Zack seemed a little perplexed by his reaction to the few words that had been scrawled on the paper. Folding it up and stuffing the paper into his shirt pocket, Clint took a dollar from another pocket and tossed it to Zack. The clerk wasn't the most coordinated man in Labyrinth, but he managed to dredge up enough agility to pluck the coin from the air.

"Thanks for rushing this over," Clint said.

Zack held the dollar in his palm as though he half expected it to be snatched away from him. "I didn't realize it was so important. I just knew you'd be here around this time, so I thought I'd save you a trip to the telegraph office."

"Predictable as ever, huh?" Clint said as a smirk returned to his face. "Actually, I'd appreciate it if you forgot what was in that message."

"Oh, I assure you I didn't pry," Zack sputtered defensively. "I'm not the type to read anyone else's—"

"I know, Zack," Clint interrupted. "Just forget what you

9

wrote. If anyone asks, it was just a message from some
gun dealers up north asking for a testimonial. Lord knows
I get enough of those to choke a horse."

Nodding, Zack closed his fingers around the dollar and
dropped the treasure deep into his trouser pocket. "Sure
thing, Mister Adams. Anything else I can do for you?"

"If you get another message like this, I'd appreciate it
if you bring it to me as quickly as possible. No matter
what time it is or what's going on. And I only want you
to deliver it, all right?"

Zack looked furtively over his shoulder at the few others
in the saloon. Even though the remaining drinkers were
either wrapped up in their own conversations or too far
away to hear what Clint had been saying, the clerk regarded them with open suspicion. "I'll be sure to do that,
Mister Adams."

"Thanks."

Taking that as his cue to leave, Zack turned and did his
best to stroll casually out of the saloon.

Hartman took Clint's mug and refilled it under the tap.
Setting it down on the bar, he said, "Mind if I ask what
that was all about?"

Clint took a healthy pull from the beer mug and let the
brew wash down his throat before answering. "It looks like
my routine is about to change."

Part of being a good friend was knowing when to talk,
when to keep quiet, and when to just turn around and leave
a man alone. Because of that, he knew for sure that it was
time to find something else to do at another part of the
saloon.

"If you need anything," Hartman said, "I'll be around."
Hartman left the bar, leaving the new bartender to fend for
himself.

Clint nodded and waited until Hartman was gone before
taking the telegram out of his pocket and unfolding it once
again. It wasn't as though he distrusted Rick. On the con-

trary, he trusted Hartman with his life. But because he was such a good friend, Clint knew it was more important that the gambler be kept out of this particular event.

Leaning against the side of the bar, Clint held his beer in one hand and the telegram in the other. He scanned the words again while thinking about what they could be leading toward.

HOPE I FOUND YOU ON MY FIRST TRY **STOP**
WILL BE ARRIVING AT TEN O'CLOCK STAGE TOMOR-
ROW **STOP**
WE HAVE IMPORTANT MATTERS TO DISCUSS **STOP**
J. WEST

Clint knew better than to think that a man like Jim West had been looking for him for too long. Being an agent of the U.S. Secret Service, West wouldn't have to look too long for anybody once he set his mind to it. In fact, Clint wondered if West wasn't already in Labyrinth and just laying low to make sure that he wasn't being followed before moving in for the upcoming meeting.

No, Clint thought. That would have been more of a job for West's partner. And if that was the case, Clint knew better than to even try looking at the faces around him because it would be next to hopeless to pick out the master of disguise.

As he finished his beer, Clint's mind raced with more concerns than he could comfortably process. Although it would be good to see West again after so many years, he knew better than to think the agent was in Texas for anything besides business. Since West normally was assigned to only the most pressing of matters, his type of business was any other man's nightmare.

And if a man like West said he has "important" matters to discuss, that brought the nightmare to a whole other level.

Clint set his mug down and tossed some money onto the bar. Striding out of the saloon, he made his way to the first newspaper he could get his hands on, bought it, and started reading through the pages as soon as he found a place to stand.

He didn't know what he was looking for, but he knew that whatever West was working on was either in the headlines or would be in print soon enough. As he scanned the various articles, Clint knew he wouldn't find anything to give him a clue as to what West could be after. In fact, Clint doubted that there were more than five or six people in the world who would know that kind of information.

To clear his mind, Clint started walking the streets of Labyrinth with the newspaper folded up beneath his arm. He thought about the endless possibilities that West could offer, until his mind began to spin. And at the core of all his thoughts, there was a strand of memories from the last time Clint had met up with Jim West.

There were bits of conversations, pieces of the few missions he'd been a part of, as well as all the wild times that came along with simply knowing a man like West. But foremost on his mind was a conversation they'd had the last time they'd parted ways.

It wasn't much more than a few sentences, but they'd stuck in Clint's brain as though they'd been glued there.

Before he knew it, Clint had walked back to the livery where he passed the time preparing Eclipse for a ride that might come at a moment's notice. Once that was done, he read through the rest of the paper, checked the timetables for the railroad, and then got something to eat. After that, he got another drink at Rick's Place and then strolled down to the train station with plenty of time to spare before the last arrival pulled up to the platform.

The sun was barely a glowing sliver on the horizon by the time the engine hissed to a stop. Rays of light stabbed into Clint's eyes with a last blaze of glory before being snuffed out by the night. As steam started to billow around the bottom of the engine like an approaching fog, the doors to the passenger cars were pulled open to allow the porters to hop down to the platform. After a few preparations were made, passengers started spilling out and making their way to the growing pile of luggage being tossed down from the baggage car.

Clint watched the new arrivals as they met up with friends or relatives, drifting away from the locomotive in a slow, steady stream. Finally, one man stepped down onto the boards, his feet planting firmly with subtle confidence.

The man strode over to Clint and tipped his hat. From a distance it had looked like Jim West, the same athletic build and good looks. The man moved with the same grace but was not, in fact, Jim West. Clint knew who he was, though, having met and worked with him on several other occasions. This was Jim West's younger cousin, Jeremy, also a member of the Secret Service.

"Adams," West said. "Good to see you. How've you been?"

"Not bad, Jeremy. Yourself?"

"You know me, Clint. Wherever I go, good times always seem to follow."

"Funny," Clint said as he shook West's hand. "But I always heard quite the opposite."

FOUR

Clint Adams and Jeremy West sat at a table in the back of Rick's Place. By the time they'd walked over there from the train station, the saloon was teeming with gamblers, drinkers, cowboys, and showgirls. Besides being the perfect place to relax after a long train ride, the saloon was the ideal place to fade away into a dark corner and be forgotten.

Holding up his half-full whiskey glass, West smiled broadly and said, "Here's to old friends."

"To old friends," Clint replied while lifting his beer mug up in toast.

Dressed in a dark blue suit that had been finely tailored to fit without giving so much as a hint to the pistol stored beneath his shoulder, West sat in the dark saloon as though he'd spent every night of his life in the place. His posture was easy and relaxed, even as his eyes casually scanned every face that fell into his field of vision. There wasn't a single part of him that looked out of place. Everything right down to the hair on his head seemed completely unaffected by the daylong train ride he'd taken to get to West Texas. He even had a way of wearing the holster around his waist without appearing to be much of a threat.

14

But Clint had worked with both Jim and Jeremy West enough to know differently. After working his way through the elite ranks of the Secret Service, Jeremy West was as dangerous as they came. The fact that he looked relatively harmless was just another weapon in the man's arsenal.

West hadn't said much of anything on their way to the saloon. That alone had been enough to warn Clint that there was most definitely a storm brewing somewhere. If it wasn't here, it was wherever Jeremy West was headed.

Both men took a swig and set their drinks down on the table. Once the whiskey had burned its trail down his throat, West nodded in admiration and leaned back in his chair. "Glad to see you remembered my cousin's code."

Clint chuckled under his breath. "There wasn't much to remember. If the letter says you're on the last stage coming into town, I should look for you on the first. Tomorrow morning's train means the last one tonight. Actually, I would think a big-time agent like yourself would be able to come up with something a little more inventive. Like maybe a different name."

West shrugged good-naturedly. "I can't get too inventive. After all, I had to think of something even a simple man like yourself wouldn't forget over the years. It's either that, or advertise my comings and goings to every telegraph office in the state before I get there."

"It's not that I'm not glad to see you, but something tells me that you're here for something else than to test my memory."

West looked around once more. The motion didn't appear to be much more than a casual shift of the eyes before speaking. When he looked around, however, West took in every detail that could be seen and measured it for any possible threat before speaking again. "Unfortunately, I'm not here for a social call. Have you been reading the papers lately?"

"Actually, I have."

"Well, if you've been keeping up on national affairs, you might have heard the name Diego Varillo mentioned once or twice in passing."

Clint nodded and took another sip of beer. "Isn't Varillo the one that's been working with the army to patch up relations between the United States and military extremists south of the border?"

"That's the one. Varillo was a colonel in the Mexican Army before he was kicked out for helping himself to the national treasury to fund his own little agenda, which included everything from murder to smuggling weapons across the border. The president down there didn't have too much of a problem until Varillo made it known that he considered himself to be an authority unto himself."

"That usually doesn't go over too well," Clint said.

"Yeah. In fact, the notion went over so badly that Varillo got kicked out of Mexico's army altogether. Unfortunately, he wasn't blowing smoke when he made his claims regarding just how much power he holds."

Clint leaned forward, suddenly feeling uncomfortable at the thought of anyone overhearing the conversation. "I never read that much in any papers. Then again, I'm not always able to keep in touch."

"Even if you read every newspaper every morning and every night, you wouldn't have heard all of this. What I'm telling you is classified information, Clint. Most of it is right off the list of things I'm not even supposed to tell you."

"All right. Definitely not a social visit," Clint said to break the tension. "I'll try not to whisper it to any drunks around here."

West, who was normally always in good spirits no matter how close the world was to burning down around him, kept a straight face and once again scanned the crowd. "The U.S. government has been dealing with Varillo on and off for years, all the way back to when he held his official rank as colonel. But once he took off on his own, Varillo has been busy playing the part of negotiator while spending the rest of his time building up his own army, which made the old extremists look like schoolchildren.

"When he started thinking he was the highest authority in Mexico, Varillo became not only a threat to their president but our own borders as well."

"That's more like what I read about him," Clint said. "If I recall, the editorial I read named him as a guerilla leader who wanted to spill American blood just to prove that Mexico is a force to be reckoned with. Some kind of revolutionary or something."

"Well, we've known about the revolutionary part for some time now. Lately, it's been the 'or something' that's had us worried."

Clint mulled that over for a second while looking toward some of the nearby card tables. For a moment, he felt as though some of West's habits had already begun to wear off on him as he started watching all the faces within eye-shot. Turning back to West, he said, "So what has all of this got to do with me? I'm pretty sure you wouldn't go through all this trouble just to fill me in on secret government information."

"You're definitely right about that. In fact, I hope you've been paying especially close attention to all of this because your memory might be put to the test."

"Is that so? Has Varillo been through here recently on some sort of invasion?"

West tossed back the rest of his drink and set the glass down in front of him. "Nope. He's been staying close to home. It's you that'll be doing the invading."

FIVE

Coming from any other man, West's last statement might have sounded impossible at best or even ludicrous at worst. When he heard the words straight from the agent's mouth, however, Clint merely nodded and finished off the rest of his beer.

"Sounds like a hell of a job," Clint said. "Do I get to hear anything else about it, or am I just supposed to volunteer?"

West studied Clint with expert eyes. Apparently satisfied with what he'd seen, the agent waved to a saloon girl and ordered another round of drinks. "I thought I'd get that part out of the way first before wasting your time with a lot of unnecessary details."

Clint put on a hurt expression. "That's not like you, Jeremy. I've always been there whenever you or Jim needed help. That's what friends are for."

"Hell, Clint, you don't have to tell me that. You've come through for us more times than most friends we've ever had. That's why I want you to know that if you don't want any part of this job, you just stop me at any time and I'll understand. But if you do decide to go through with it . . . you'll be in it up to your ears."

Hartman walked over and set the drinks down on the table. He seemed ready to make some small talk himself, but after only a second or two he could feel the tense seriousness hanging over the table like a shroud. Deciding to simply leave the two alone to finish whatever business they'd started, the barkeep excused himself and tended to the hundred other things requiring his attention.

Reading the face of the man in front of him, Clint barely even noticed that Hartman had already come and gone.

"So what do you think so far?" West asked. "Still interested?"

"Keep talking. We'll see how interested I get."

After sampling the whiskey, West set his elbows on the table and stared Clint straight in the eyes. "In public, Varillo's been acting as a middleman for negotiations to try and make things easier in the trouble spots along the border. In private, he's been calling for revolution and has done so ever since he's had people around him who would listen."

"Mexico's full of men like that," Clint said. "I've met plenty of them myself."

"True enough. But Mexico isn't full of men who can actually back up what they say."

"And Varillo can?"

West nodded. "Despite the troubles he's had with the president down there, he's still got enough pull inside the Mexican government to attract our attention. Also, he's drawn enough followers to form an army of his own that also has contacts in the smuggling trade, which adds up to one hell of a well-equipped band of radicals with a powerful man stoking the fires beneath them."

"Hasn't the army known about this before now?" Clint asked. "I mean, how could a man like this become so powerful without being taken down already by someone like . . . well . . . you?"

West got a genuine laugh out of that. "I'm kept pretty

busy. In fact, I have crossed paths with Varillo once or twice earlier in his career." Suddenly, some of the gloom that had settled over West's face was pushed away by a familiar glint in his eye. "Actually," he said while leaning in a little closer, "there was this time in Mexico City when . . ." Catching himself before committing to the story, West stopped short and leaned back in his chair. "Let's just say he's been put into check a couple of times. The only problem is that he lays low just long enough to lick his wounds and doesn't resurface again until he's stronger than he was before.

"It's been a few years since he went into hiding last time. And since then, he's covered his tracks well enough to be forgotten. There have been rumors about his movements, but nothing big enough to warrant an investigation."

Clint shook his head. "You're a great friend, Jeremy. Your only problem is that you and Jim never come by just to shoot the bull and have a drink. Every time we get together, I wind up getting thrown into a meat grinder."

West's face twisted into a little smile. "As much as I'd like to say otherwise, this might just be one of those times. Right now, I'm working on a case in California so I won't be able to have much of a part in this Varillo problem."

"And what about Jim and his partner?"

"Actually, they're both out of the country on separate assignments."

"And here it comes," Clint said while preparing himself for the knockout punch.

"Varillo's forces were spotted by a cavalry troop moving west less than a week ago. That would put their position approximately directly south of here in less than a day. That is, of course, as long as they haven't decided to change direction."

"Or if they didn't allow themselves to be spotted just to throw you off the trail."

Smiling broadly, West pointed a finger at Clint and said, "That, my friend, is exactly why I thought of you for this job. You think on your feet, you can handle yourself in a scrape, and you know this part of the country like the back of your hand."

"What about other agents?" Clint asked. "Aren't there any others working in the Service or did they whittle it down to just you, Jim, and his partner?"

Deciding to ignore that last question, West turned in his seat to take notice of something going on in another part of the room. When Clint finally turned to see what had caught his friend's attention, he found a particularly busty saloon girl leaning over a poker table to wish one of the players luck. Clint knew better than to try and pull West away from a sight like that and after a moment or two, he even found himself drawn into the woman's bouncing movements.

After the girl straightened up and lost herself in the crowd, West turned back around to face Clint. "There was something else that made me think of you for this job. Something that made it particularly suited to your . . . expertise."

"Uh-oh," Clint said. "You're using the big words. That's never good."

"The Service managed to get a hold of one of Varillo's men during a smuggling run that was ambushed by Texas Rangers a few weeks ago. He didn't say much, but he let it slip that Varillo is hiring all the men he can get his hooks into. He's already got plenty of equipment and now he's after some real talent."

"Gunmen?"

"More than that," West said in a lower voice. "Killers. Sharpshooters. Assassins. Combine them with a well-equipped army positioning itself around our borders and you've got a whole mess of trouble that we never expected even from someone like Varillo."

"You're talking about a real invasion here," Clint said.

"Yeah. That's exactly what I'm talking about."

"How close is Varillo to actually pulling off something like that?"

West held up his hands. "This information hasn't been around too long. We've only just put it all together. Although there's no official estimate, I'd say that Varillo must be damn close if he's even poking his head out far enough for us to spot him. I've met the man. I know he's got the ambition to think big enough for something like this. Up until now, the only thing saving him from being a more important target was the fact that he never had the means."

"Until now," Clint stated.

"That's right. Until now."

"But does he really have enough men, guns, and power to pose a threat to the United States?"

"As far as we can tell . . . no. Dealing with the military and politics is like standing in a warehouse full of dynamite. Varillo might not be strong enough to make a bigger explosion than us, but he might just be able to force his way close enough to a powder keg and set off a spark or two. After that . . ."

West didn't have to finish his statement. The point had been made, and suddenly the dark cloud that had been hanging over the table got a little darker.

SIX

Gerard Lantiss stood at the bar inside Rick's Place, wedged in between two drunks who insisted on talking to him no matter how many times he tried to shrug them off. Once he started nodding and pretending to listen to the drunks, however, they quieted down enough to provide excellent cover amid the backdrop of the teeming saloon.

Dressed in expensive yet conservative attire, he was just distinguished enough to maintain his dignity, yet not impressive enough to stand out in the crowd. His dark burgundy jacket was only buttoned loosely at the bottom so his white linen shirt could be seen beneath the colorful material. The gun he wore was a pearl-handled .38 riding high on his hip so that only the bottom of its barrel poked down from the cover of his jacket. Plain black pants gave way to polished riding boots.

Like a coiled serpent, he only moved when it was absolutely necessary. Whenever the drunks on either side of him forced him to shift on his feet, he glared at them with a quick trace of disgust. That, however, was only a flicker across his face, soon to be replaced by the mask worn for social occasions.

He didn't have to add anything to the conversation or

23

even look at the drunks for them to keep right on talking
and slapping him on the back every once in a while at the
end of their stories. That was all well and good since the
reason for Lantiss being in the bar, or in West Texas, was
sitting at a table in the opposite corner.

Peering out of the corner of his eye, Lantiss focused on
Jeremy West's back as though he was sighting down the
barrel of his custom-made Winchester rifle. It was obvious
that West could sense that he was being watched. Whenever the Secret Service agent would turn to look for the
eyes that were burning holes in the back of his head, Lantiss would merely duck behind his drunken companions
and suddenly become more interested in whatever it was
they were saying.

Instinctively, Lantiss could tell when the Service agent
went back to his conversation. This time, when he turned
to look at West's table, Lantiss paid closer attention to the
man sitting across from the agent. Of course Lantiss recognized the face, but he couldn't help but be surprised at
the fact that West had chosen this particular contact at all.

After letting another couple of minutes pass by, Lantiss
stepped away from the bar and let his space get filled almost instantly by a local who was closer to the level of
intoxication of Lantiss's former neighbors.

The saloon was alive and pulsing with the thump of feet
against floorboards, raised voices, and the tinny patter of
a piano. Keeping his head low, Lantiss made his way
through the crowd. He was careful not to assert himself
too much, so he could avoid drawing any more attention
to himself than was necessary.

Sliding like a shark's fin through the sea of bodies, Lantiss maneuvered deftly toward the tables occupied by gamblers and covered by multicolored chips. He stepped up
behind one of the observers near a high-stakes game and
leaned in close to her ear.

"You didn't tell me that Clint Adams would be here,"

he hissed so that only the smiling brunette could hear.

Keeping the well-practiced beaming expression on her face, the woman made sure not to take her eyes away from the table. "I'm not a census taker, Gerard."

Leaning down a little lower, the brunette allowed everyone at the table as well as a good portion of the room a good, lingering look down he front of her low-cut dress. Once she was certain that nobody was paying attention to anything but her cleavage, she took a look at the cards held by the man to her right, memorized them, and then straightened up again.

Lantiss was still there when she turned around.

"Follow me," he said with a cold smile. "We have some catching up to do."

His hand latched onto her forearm in a chilling embrace. After more than one try, she still wasn't able to pull away. Although she shot a warning glare at him, it didn't have enough real conviction behind it to hide the fear she felt in his presence. "Just a moment," she insisted. "I'm not through here just yet."

Lantiss let his eyes roam over the woman and then the table in front of her. Still maintaining his casual demeanor, he nodded and said, "Fine. Just be quick about it."

Only after gripping her arm tight enough to send a jolt of pain up to her shoulder did Lantiss unlock his fingers. He held her gaze for another second, which was more than enough to send his message slithering beneath her skin.

The woman stood her ground as Lantiss moved away. As much as her arm hurt, she refused to give him the satisfaction of seeing her rub it or even wince with discomfort. Instead, she kept her relaxed façade up and worked her way around the table until she was behind one of the older, more rotund players of the game.

Once again, she flipped her hair over her shoulders and leaned down to give the other half of the room its show while placing her lips against the player's ear. Using only

a few quick words, she told the gambler what his oppo-
nents were holding and then kissed him affectionately on
the cheek. Just to put the few minds that weren't occupied
by her body to rest, she went over to the others at the table
and kissed them as well, whispering, "Good luck, hand-
some," into their ears just loud enough for the others not
to hear.

Turning on her heel, she faced away from the table and
walked across the room in a flurry of blue and green silk
skirts. On the way over to where Lantiss was standing, she
made a quick estimate of the money she'd seen spread out
on that table, figuring the percentage she'd be receiving
from the old man for helping him "win" it.

The warm feeling of victory that had been settling into
her quickly dissipated, however, when she saw Lantiss's
hard green eyes fixing on her as she drew closer. They
were positioned near the edge of the room close to the
back. Lantiss had his shoulders almost touching the wall
and his hands crossed imperiously over his chest.

"My dear," he said, his voice cutting through every
other noise in the room like a stiletto through smooth flesh,
"you have got a lot of explaining to do."

SEVEN

The last few moments had passed in silence. Even with the organized chaos inside the saloon, the table shared by Clint and Jeremy West seemed to be disturbingly quiet. West's last unfinished statement loomed in the air like a specter over their heads.

"So what this all boils down to," Clint said, "is the threat of war."

"Potentially . . . yes. If Varillo kicks up enough dirt and plays his cards right, he might just be able to drag the governments of Mexico and the Unites States into a fight."

"But if our government already knows what Varillo is doing . . ."

"Doesn't matter," West said sharply. "If tensions escalate past a certain point, all it will take is a shot fired in the wrong direction or a soldier getting killed by the wrong army and the whole mess goes up in smoke."

Clint soaked this in for a second while nursing his beer. After looking around at the saloon and all the people inside of it for a bit, he turned back to West and shook his head. "You're not telling me something, Jeremy."

"If you're wondering how you fit in to all of this, then—"

"No," Clint interrupted. "Before that. If all of this can lead to something as big as war between the United States and Mexico, how come you haven't taken care of it already? Why bother with a civilian rather than one of the other agents? And don't feed me that same line about how talented I am and how well I know the area."

For a second, West actually looked insulted. He lowered his eyes as though he was genuinely disappointed by what Clint had said. When he looked up again, there was that familiar glint in his eye that was the man's real feeling showing through. "All right," he said. "As always, you know me a little too well."

Leaning forward to place both arms on the table, he locked eyes with Clint and asked, "You ever hear of the Ghost Squadron?"

Clint searched his memory for a second or two before shrugging. "Can't say as I have."

"Well, if you'd have answered yes to that question, I would have accused you of lying or suspected you'd taken up a government job of your own. The Ghost Squadron is a cavalry unit headed up by a lieutenant by the name of Muller. Once a soldier proves himself to the higher-ups and joins Lieutenant Muller's squad, they become officially dead and are never heard from again.

"They're used mainly for infiltration and demolition work. Not to mention the occasional assassination whenever it's needed. They don't have a permanent base, the dossier on their ranks would be hard to get even if I needed it, and their jobs usually all play a pivotal role in national security."

"Don't tell me that Varillo managed to get a hold of this squad," Clint said.

"Not at all. On the contrary, the Ghosts have just been sent down to the border to get inside Varillo's platoon and tear it up from the inside. But since the colonel managed to keep his head down until the last possible minute, they don't have enough time to establish cover and safely plant somebody inside Varillo's camp."

"So why not just take them all out?" Clint asked. "If this Ghost Squadron is that good, they should be able to raid a band of revolutionaries, right?"

"Given enough time to gather intelligence and scout things out . . . sure. But this platoon moving north toward Texas could just be a fragment of Varillo's army and the leader of the Ghosts doesn't want to risk it. Hitting them could only postpone the colonel's invasion as well as warn him that he's being watched. If that happens, he might not surface again until he's marching through Dallas."

"And that, I suppose, is where I come in?"

Nodding, West said, "Exactly." He lifted his glass in a silent toast and downed the remains of his whiskey.

"Okay, Jeremy. You've got my interest. Let's hear the good stuff."

"To put it simply, Lieutenant Muller needs some way to get in good with Varillo's men damn quick. Varillo is looking for gunfighters and men to lend some serious credibility to his army among the killer and smuggler circuit that money just can't buy.

"All someone like the Gunsmith would have to do is ride in, convince Varillo that he was on the level, and pick his rank among the invaders." West still ran his fingers around he edge of his shot glass. His posture was relaxed and confident, but his eyes betrayed the nervousness he was feeling.

"And what's the downside?" Clint asked, spotting the hint of tension hidden inside West's features.

Letting out a breath, West gave up on trying to hide his concern. "One slipup and he or his men will do their best to kill you. Besides having plenty of killers in his ranks already, he's got sheer numbers on his side. Also . . . and this is just strictly my own theory here . . . I think there might just be someone in the Ghost Squadron who already signed up for the wrong side."

Since Clint hadn't been feeling too good about any of this to begin with, that last little tidbit actually didn't hit him too hard. On top of everything else, it was just one more thing to worry about grouped in with a thousand others.

"I know this is a lot to think about all at once," West said. "And I don't expect an answer from you right away."

Smiling, Clint asked, "How long do I have to think it over?"

"Oh . . . about twelve hours."

Clint nodded. "That's pretty much what I thought."

"Look, I wouldn't even ask you to do this if I didn't think you could pull it off. You're a good friend and have come through for me plenty of times. If this wasn't so damn important, I never would consider putting you in this kind of trouble. If it helps any, I'll have you know that the Service is willing to pay—"

"I'm sure the money will be fine," Clint said offhandedly. "All I need to know is one thing."

"Name it."

"When can I meet Lieutenant Muller?"

EIGHT

"Tell me something, Rebecca," Lantiss said. "How much longer did you think you could keep taking the colonel's money without giving back anything in return?"

Rebecca ran her fingers through her long dark hair and let her nails drift down over her breasts. "I've given plenty for the few dollars you threw my way."

"Oh, spare me. You've proven to be nothing but an overpriced whore who occasionally catches a bit of information. You know more than you tell. At least to me, anyway, which concerns me greatly."

"I report everything I hear. It's not my fault if there hasn't been much going on lately."

Lantiss's eyes flicked over to where Jeremy West was sitting with his back to them. The motion was barely a hint of movement, but was enough to draw Rebecca's attention. "I suppose you call the arrival of Clint Adams as nothing worth mentioning?" he asked.

"I've had my eye on him. So far, he's only left town once or twice, but other than that he's spent his days without so much as getting drunk."

"Now is not the time to hold back," Lantiss snarled. "If you've got something else to say, you'd best say it now.

Otherwise, if I have to find it out for myself, I'll gut you so slowly the last thing you'll hear is the sound of your flesh tearing apart."

If Rebecca was affected by Lantiss's threat, she did a good job of hiding it. Her eyes were devoid of emotion and never once turned away from the man sitting across from her. Even the way her body was situated in the chair seemed aloof and collected.

"Did you have anything else to tell me," she said, "or were you just stopping by to give me a scare?"

Lantiss might very well have been carved out of the side of a glacier. Fixing his eyes upon her, he didn't so much as blink until a full two minutes had passed. Finally, he said, "You know damn well I should have known about Adams being here the minute he arrived. Errors like that make me wonder if you knew about West's arrival."

"Adams comes and goes here in Labyrinth," she argued. "It's no big news when he comes to town."

Reaching under his jacket, Lantiss brushed his fingers over the small holster strapped beneath his shoulder. He lingered over the smooth leather for a second before probing into an inside pocket to retrieve a small canvas pouch. "Here," he said while tossing the pouch onto the table. "This should cover your fee for the next couple of weeks. Start earning it by moving over to West's table over there and distracting him. Adams, too."

Rebecca picked up the pouch, weighed it in the palm of her hand, and held it by the drawstrings. "Which one do you want dead?"

Lantiss arched his eyebrows. "So eager to start earning your keep? Are you certain you can handle either of them?"

Getting up from her chair, Rebecca stepped over to Lantiss's side with the canvas pouch dangling between her fingers. Slowly, she bent at the waist until she could lift the hem of her dress and pull it up over her leg while straightening her back. Once the material was up high enough to expose her left leg almost to the point where it met her hips, she eased the material aside and hooked her thumb beneath a black garter resting around the middle of her thigh.

In one flicker of motion, she tucked the top half of the pouch beneath the garter and kept her thigh on display for a second before easing her fingers away. The dress slid down her leg and came to a rest on top of her feet.

"I can handle anything," she whispered. "You'd be smart to remember that the next time you want to try and threaten me like I'm nothing but another one of Varillo's mistresses."

The two locked eyes. Although it only lasted a few seconds, the quiet power struggle held enough tension to ignite the air flowing between them. It was Lantiss who broke off first, pushing away from the table and getting to his feet.

Looking down at her as though he was perched upon a ten-foot pedestal, Lantiss allowed an amused smirk to crawl onto his face. "Posture all you want, sweet Rebecca. But don't take too long at it. You've still got a job to do."

Rebecca watched the man leave and then turned to look at the table being occupied by Clint Adams and Jeremy West. Figuring that she'd already attracted enough attention by her little display moments ago, she put on the face she wore to conduct business, tossed her hair back, and sauntered back into the crowd.

NINE

"Lieutenant Muller is riding up from the border tonight. You can meet with him tomorrow afternoon at a little town called Perro Rojo. He's actually quite excited to make your acquaintance."

Clint couldn't help but laugh. "News sure travels fast with you people. I only just accepted this job a minute ago."

"Yeah, well something told me that you wouldn't pass this one up. Not when there was so much at stake. Besides, you've never let me down before."

Holding up his empty beer mug, Clint said, "Here's to making big assumptions. Speaking of which, the rest of tonight's drinks are on you."

"I have no problem with that. After all, I couldn't have you going into something like this sober, now could I?"

Clint sat back and let West fetch the next round of drinks. After the agent returned, the two men started talking about everything else that didn't have to do with official government affairs. It was good to be able to catch up after all the time that had passed since the last time his path had crossed West's and the next half hour flew by like a heartbeat. It didn't take long to forget all the thoughts of war and revolution once both men were knee-deep in memories and bawdy anecdotes.

Their spirits were at their peak when Clint noticed a beautiful set of eyes staring back at him from the next table. Even in the dim light of the saloon, Clint could see the rich, dark brown depths taking him in with undisguised hunger. He recognized her immediately as the brunette who'd been standing with the gamblers on the other side of the room.

As soon as she saw that she'd been noticed, the woman turned up the corners of her mouth and walked to the table with such smooth steps that her feet barely seemed to touch the floor. She settled into a chair between Clint and West, crossed her legs, and held out her hand.

"I'm Rebecca Chase," she said in a low, sultry voice. "Mind if I join you?"

West took her hand and kissed it delicately. "Not at all, ma'am. In fact, I would be quite heartbroken if you decided to leave."

Rolling his eyes at the other man's honey-coated demeanor, Clint nodded to Rebecca. "Please excuse my over-enthusiastic friend, Miss Chase. Sometimes it's hard to tell which he's more full of . . . himself or whiskey." When he saw her laugh at the comment, Clint followed it up by offering his own hand. "My name's Clint Adams."

Once she got her hand free from West, she took Clint's and squeezed his just enough to transfer some of the warmth from her skin into Clint's flesh. Rebecca held onto him for a second and then looked deeply into Clint's eyes. When she blinked, she displayed a long set of eyelashes that batted at the air like butterfly wings.

"Pleased to meet you, Clint," she said. "I've heard an awful lot about you."

"Nothing bad, I hope."

"That's a little too much to ask for," West jibed. "But we can at least hope she hasn't heard the really bad things."

Again, Rebecca laughed while looking down at the table. This close to her, Clint could smell the spicy scent of her skin. She smelled like exotic spices mixed with the natural, delicious odor of a woman.

"No need to fight over me," she said while sliding the top corners of her dress down so that they were even with the garment's neckline. "There's plenty to go around."

Clint had seen plenty of showgirls work for their next client, but he still couldn't help but be impressed by the intoxicating display Rebecca was giving them. Her skin was smooth and richly tanned all down her neck and along the slope of her breasts. Peeking just above the material, however, was the start of more pale flesh that didn't normally see the light of day. The contrast of light and dark only drew Clint's eyes further over her body, making him wonder if the creamier skin felt any different after being wrapped in silk and lace all day long.

Leaning in closer to Clint's side of the table, Rebecca put her hand on top of his and held on gently. "I've heard that you've been in town for a while. Some of the other girls talk about you, but I'm not used to believing a word they say." Her eyes drifted down over Clint's chest and then a ways lower. "Now that I see you for myself, I'm sure that they couldn't have been lying about everything."

West chuckled to himself. "I wouldn't be too hasty, miss. Sometimes your first instincts are the ones that serve you the best."

Glancing across the table, Clint was just in time to see the smug look on West's face. The expression was quickly followed up by a mischievous wink from the agent. "Do us both a favor, Jeremy. Why don't you get Rebecca something to drink and we can all continue this conversation? That is, if we're still here when you get back."

Rebecca's eyes burned when she heard that last part and she moistened her upper lip with the tip of her tongue. Squeezing Clint's hand subtly, she nodded and looked to

West. "That sounds wonderful. I'll have something to cool me down. I trust you won't get me anything too strong."

"Don't you worry," West said as he got up and tipped his hat. "I live to serve." Giving Clint a pat on the shoulder as he walked by, West worked his way across the room, found himself a place at the bar, and waited there for a bit before even attempting to get Hartman's attention.

"I hope your friend wasn't too angry," Rebecca said once West had gone.

"Don't worry about him. He's used to things like that happening whenever we get together." Clint managed to keep a straight face for a full second before they both broke into comfortable laughter.

Standing near the front door of the saloon, Lantiss nodded to himself as he watched the body language of Clint Adams and Rebecca at the far side of the room. He held up his left hand and twitched his fingers, which brought two men instantly to his side.

"Looks like the bitch is good for something after all," Lantiss said to the man closest to him. "The targets are separated. I want half of you to go after West and the other half to go after Adams. I'll be ready to back up whichever team needs it."

Turning to look at the slender gunman, Lantiss added, "Nothing fancy. Just get close to them, kill them, and get out. Anyone gets in your way . . . put a bullet through their skull. Any questions?"

The killers didn't need to know anything else.

TEN

Rick Hartman spotted West standing at the bar and recognized him as the man who'd been talking to Clint for a good part of the night. Knowing better than to ask about the topic of their conversation, Hartman stepped up next to West and smiled broadly. "Rick Hartman. I own the place."

"Jeremy West." The two shook hands.

"Need another round for your table?" Rick asked.

"I'm doing all right, myself," West replied. "But maybe you could suggest something for our new friend over there."

Hartman looked to where West was pointing. "Ah. I see you've met Rebecca."

"We sure have. Does she work here?"

"No, but she does come here quite often. Mostly she stays close to the gamblers. If this is about someone cheated out of their money, then I'll be sure to have one of my boys pull her out of—"

"No, no," West interrupted. "Nothing so drastic. I'm just making sure she's not some character I need to keep an eye on. After all, I am new in town."

Hartman thought it over for a second or two and then

shrugged. "Can't say as I know of anything too bad about her. At least," he added with a conspiratorial wink, "nothing that you couldn't accuse any woman of, if you know what I mean."

Thinking back to his years in the Secret Service, West sampled only a few of the memories associated with beautiful women and the trouble that all too often went along with them. "Yeah. I think I know what you mean."

Sensing the dark turn in West's mood, Hartman slapped his hands together and rubbed them vigorously. "So, what can I get for ya? I know Clint Adams pretty well, myself, and he never has much trouble with the ladies. I know just the thing to help relax her a bit."

"Something with some bite to it," West suggested. "Let's see what our sweet Rebecca is made of."

"I know just the thing." And with that, Hartman turned around quickly and had a few words with the bartender, who then began plucking bottles off the shelf behind them and splashing their contents into a small metal mixing cup.

West watched Clint's table from the corner of his eye. There was something that had set off a vague sense of danger that nagged at the back of his head like a fly buzzing behind his ear. Although he couldn't put his finger on exactly what it was, he was reluctant to dismiss the feeling. Mainly because that insistent buzzing had saved his life more often than he could count.

Suddenly, the hairs on the back of his neck stood on end. West's first impulse was to turn and face Clint's table so he could try to pick out any signs of trouble that might be coming from that area. Just when he thought he'd gotten a little too paranoid, he spotted a group of three men working their way through the crowd, coming straight behind Clint's chair.

"Here you go, Mister West," Hartman said as he set the concoction he'd mixed up onto the bar in front of the agent. "This should go over pretty well with the lady."

West turned to the gambler only for a second, doing his best to keep the group of men in the edge of his field of vision. "Get the law down here," he said quickly. "And be ready for—"

In the next instant, that persistent rattle in the back of West's mind kicked up to the mental equivalent of a freight train steaming through his skull. Reflexively, his hand snapped toward the handle of his gun as every muscle in his body clenched in anticipation of the worst.

It was sheer instinct that allowed West to duck at the last second, narrowly avoiding the slim dagger being thrust at his neck. The blade whistled through the air, taking with it a thin shaving of West's flesh as it went by. A tiny rivulet of blood dripped onto the agent's tailored collar, bringing an angry sneer to his lips.

West twisted at the waist while bringing up his right fist and burying it into the gut of the man who'd tried to stab him. His knuckles slammed into solid muscle, but rather than be intimidated, West followed up with a sharp left jab and then another right to the same spot.

Like chipping away at a tree trunk, West's blows finally started to affect his attacker. The bigger man crumpled slightly and stepped back. In less than half a second, his spot was filled by another man squaring off with West. This one, however, was clutching a pistol instead of a knife.

West gritted his teeth and committed himself to the fray, hoping that he'd made enough noise to give Clint at least some kind of warning as to what was coming his way.

It didn't take Clint long to realize that nearly everything Rebecca said was laced with some kind of innuendo or flirtatious double meaning. Her voice was almost addictive in its rich tone and the more Clint listened to her, the more he wanted to hear.

He was just about to suggest moving their conversation

to a more quiet location when he heard something coming
from the direction of the bar. The noise wasn't much when
combined with all the others floating through the saloon.
But then Clint heard the unmistakable sound of feet scuf-
fling on the floor and bodies slamming into solid wood.

Hoping that West had managed to keep himself out of
trouble for once, Clint turned in his seat just to make sure
that his friend wasn't the one causing the commotion.
More than that, he also wanted to be sure Jeremy didn't
need any help.

The pistol flashed in Clint's eye like a mirror catching
a ray of sun. Even though it hadn't been anything but a
flicker of firelight glinting off metal, the sight was enough
to put all of Clint's reflexes on the alert.

"Get down," he said to Rebecca while leaping to his
feet and putting himself between her and the incoming
gun.

Clint's hand was a blur of motion as it flashed to his
side and wrapped around the handle of the modified Colt
waiting for him inside its holster. Without taking his eyes
from the gun being held by a man dressed in shabby denim
and a dusty hat pushed down low over his brow, Clint
drew the Colt and brought it up. Although he was supremely confident in his own speed, he wasn't stupid
enough to assume he could beat a man who'd already
drawn.

Sure enough, as if to prove his fears correct, the man
with the gun stepped off slightly to the side and squeezed
his trigger. The pistol in his hand let out a thunderous blast
and sprayed a shower of sparks into the smoky air.

Clint's body was already in motion, however, reacting
in anticipation of the gunshot. Knowing that this man
wasn't interested in a fair fight, Clint knew the first shot
would be coming any second and had already acted accordingly. His left arm wrapped around Rebecca's upper

body and pulled her in close so she would be carried along as he threw himself to the side.

The bullet snapped through the air inches away from Clint's back. All that saved him was the haste in which it had been fired. When he didn't see a spray of blood or hear a cry of pain, the gunman snapped back the hammer of his pistol and took more careful aim. By the look on his face, he wasn't about to make the same mistake again.

Lantiss eased his way through the crowd as the fights began. The more excited the people around him became, the easier it was to go unnoticed. He wore a grim smile as he worked up closer to his unsuspecting target.

ELEVEN

The man with a blade clenched in one meaty fist was still reeling back from the blows West had delivered to his midsection. Instinctively, he'd then searched for the next opponent since he knew better than to think that this was the work of a single man who'd gotten a wild hair in the wrong place.

West spotted the gunman just as he stepped out of the crowd and started going for his pistol. Letting his reflexes take over, West ducked down low and threw himself out of the direct line of fire. Luckily for him, the crowd around the bar had begun to thin out the moment they sensed a fight brewing so close to them.

Gunshots blasted through the air, but they weren't quite close enough to be coming from the man he'd only just spotted. Instead, he guessed they were coming from the vicinity of Clint's table. Now, more than ever, he knew he had to get back to his friend's side to at least even up the odds somewhat.

All of these thoughts flashed through West's mind in the space of a heartbeat. As they did, his body went through the motions of drawing his pistol and finding a good position from which to fire. Another shot cracked inside the saloon. This time, it was close enough to rattle West's eardrums. The scent of freshly burned gunpowder stung the agent's nostrils.

Pivoting his body to aim at the gunman he'd spotted, West discovered that not only was that man gone, but so was the one who'd been carrying the knife. He knew better than to stop moving even for a second, so West coiled his legs beneath the rest of his body and launched himself toward a nearby table at the precise moment that not one, but two gunshots exploded no more than ten feet away from him.

West kept himself in a low crouch. In one swift motion, he dropped down to one side, broke his fall at the last moment with his hand, and lashed out with his right leg to sweep the stand out from under the table, knocking it over to provide him with a temporary shield against the next wave of bullets.

The table was still rolling to one side when a pair of slugs punched into the circular piece of lumber. But the wood was just thick enough to keep the lead from drilling all the way through, causing West to let out a small, re- lieved breath.

Snapping back the hammer of his pistol, West took up position behind the table and poked his head around the side. With the crowd retreating farther back toward the doors, the agent didn't have as hard of a time picking out the men who were trying to ambush him. They moved like professionals; quick and instinctive. But when one of them spotted West's head at the edge of the table, he stopped for a second to point him out to his partners.

West didn't hesitate for a moment before sighting down the barrel of his gun and squeezing the trigger. The weapon bucked against his palm and a dark spout of blood popped in the gunman's chest. Managing to keep his feet beneath him for a second or two, the attacker tried to take another shot, but his strength was pouring out of him in a thick, red stream.

The instant West saw movement from another part of the room, he ducked back behind the table. Some more shots were fired, but only one of them was aimed at him, taking a sizeable chunk from the edge of the table as it whipped by overhead. West cursed beneath his breath, knowing that Clint was in trouble. Even though he knew his friend could hold his own, it didn't make it any easier listening to him getting shot at.

Just then, he heard the sound of footsteps clomping on the floorboards, approaching his position. An idea formed in West's mind and he pushed his back up against the table, making sure his feet were firmly planted on the floor with his knees bent all the way up to his chin.

When he heard the steps get a little closer, he tensed the muscles in his legs.

Just a little closer . . .

With one powerful surge of energy, West grabbed hold of the post nailed to the bottom of the table while shoving his body back with every bit of force his legs could muster. Although he wasn't able to lift the table too high off the floor using just his left hand, he managed to get it just about an inch or two off the ground, which was just enough to drive it straight into the shins of the man approaching him, causing the attacker to cry out in pain.

West let the table slip from his fingers, smiling in satisfaction as it dropped heavily onto the second gunman's toes. When he stood up, West came face to face with the gunman whose features were twisted into a mask of painful surprise.

Spinning his pistol around to grab it by the barrel, West cocked his arm back and prepared to send the butt of his weapon crashing down onto the gunman's collarbone. As soon as his arm went all the way back, however, he felt the press of cold steel against his throat.

He didn't have to have eyes in the back of his head for West to picture the filthy smile on the face of the big man holding the blade. What stung the agent even worse was the fact that he'd allowed the original attacker to sneak up close enough to get the drop on him.

TWELVE

For a brief second, Clint wondered if he should simply keep the men who'd ambushed him and Rebecca busy until West could get around behind them. That flash of hope was snuffed out as fast as it had been born when he heard the sounds of an escalating battle raging near West's section of the bar.

"Get out of here," he said to Rebecca as he made sure that she was able to put some distance between herself and the attackers. "There's a back door to your—"

"I know where it is," she said breathlessly. "But I don't want to just leave you here."

Clint felt the hot sting of pain from the tear in his flesh left behind by the previous bullet. He used the pain to fuel his movements as he straightened up, spun around, and faced off with whoever was trying to kill him. "Go!" he shouted to Rebecca.

As much as she wanted to stay, Rebecca flinched at the sound of Clint's raging voice and hurried away in response to it.

Once Clint knew she'd given him some space to maneuver safely, he stepped slowly around the tables like a tiger stalking around its prey. The man who'd taken the

shots at him had already ducked down behind the end of
the bar. From what he could see, there were at least two
others positioning themselves nearby. Clint knew that if
they were allowed to get dug in too well, they might just
be able to pick him off.

As if they were thinking along the same lines, two of
the gunmen who were moving around the card tables stood
up at the same time and squeezed off a couple of rounds
in Clint's direction.

Reflexively, Clint ducked down and moved away from
them. The moment his mind caught up to his body, however, he realized that he was moving in the exact direction
his attackers had been planning on.

Rather than change direction in mid-step, Clint kept
moving toward the bar while dropping down to throw himself into a quick forward roll. Although he was a far cry
from being an acrobat, Clint managed to pull off the maneuver well enough to avoid getting hit by the first two
hastily fired rounds and land with the right end facing up
in approximately the spot he'd been hoping to hit.

Coming to a stop behind and to the right of the gunman
squatting at the end of the bar, Clint pushed himself up
off the floor the moment he was able. Gunshots echoed
through the entire saloon. There were so many now that it
was hard for Clint to pin down which were being fired at
him and which were coming from West's end of the room.
But details like that had to be pushed aside for the moment
in order for Clint to keep his body moving just perfectly
for him to stay alive.

"Hello there," Clint said to the surprised-looking gunman who spun around in an attempt to draw a bead on his
swiftly moving target.

The gunman wheeled around with his pistol held in tight
against his body. Although his movements were smooth
and efficient, he simply wasn't fast enough to track Clint,
who was managing to stay inches ahead of the pistol's

sights while dashing for the cover of the bar.

When he finally made it behind the bar, Clint twisted his body in one last burst of speed, pulling his trigger as he reached the end of the motion. The Colt barked once amid the chaotic jumble of background noise, but the single shot seemed to be the only thing either of the two men could hear.

For a second, the gunman struggled to point his weapon at Clint. But his body just didn't seem willing to cooperate. When he looked down as though searching for an explanation, he could find no sign of a wound or even a scratch. Then the blood trickled down his face and dripped off his chin. His eyes rolled up in their sockets, pointing toward the small black hole in his forehead as the rest of his body simply fell over and landed with a thump on the floor.

Placing himself in their position, Clint knew what the other two gunmen would be expecting him to do. Rather than dive for cover behind the safety of the solid oak bar, he merely faked such a motion while watching the section of tables from the corner of his eye.

Sure enough, the remaining two attackers surged forward, breaking from their cover just long enough for Clint to spot the tops of their heads. He aimed the Colt as though he was simply pointing his finger, squeezing the trigger the moment he'd pointed to where he wanted the bullet to go. The gun barked once and the gunman closest to him snapped back and slammed against the floor as though he'd been mule-kicked in the nose.

Although Clint wasn't certain whether the last gunman would run for cover or make a desperate charge, he knew that if this thing was going to end in his favor, it had to end quickly. Placing one hand on top of the bar and pushing while jumping up with both legs, Clint nearly flew over the oak structure and landed solidly on the other side.

The gunman was already bearing down on him like a runaway stagecoach, his teeth bared and his head lowered in an oncoming charge. His shoulder slammed into Clint's gut with enough force to drive the air from his lungs.

Clint had less than a second to prepare himself for the blow and managed to tighten the muscles in his stomach enough to keep him from getting all the oxygen driven out of his chest. Pain shot through his lower back as his spine crashed against the edge of the bar.

Steeling himself against the murky haze that had begun to creep in around the edge of his vision, Clint pounded the Colt's handle against the gunman's shoulder blade. He didn't wait to see how badly the other man was hurt by the blow. Instead, Clint made sure to push the man down with his arm across his back and then brought up his right knee with a snap that was followed by the sound of cartilage and bone crunching together.

The gunman's arms wrapped loosely around Clint's waist, but the movement was nothing more than a twitching reflex. In the following second, his body fell face first onto the floor.

Clint spun around to see how West was doing. At first, all he could see was a grinning face and a swiftly approaching fist. After that, he was in so much blinding pain that he thought his skull might explode as that fist made sudden contact with his nose.

Staggering back, Clint started to bring up the Colt.

"I wouldn't," Lantiss said as he tapped the barrel of his .38 against Clint's forehead.

The fog of pain was burning off inside Clint's head, but he didn't have to see a thing to recognize the fact that he was in some serious trouble. He held his Colt at his side, but in his current position, he doubted he was fast enough to fire and keep from getting his head hollowed out in the process.

Lantiss's lips curled up as his smug grin became a beaming, victorious smile. Pushing Clint back using the gun against his head, he moved them into a clearer spot on the floor. Without glancing at the gun in Clint's hand, he said, "It takes a wise man to know when he's beaten."

"Are you going to tell me why all of this is happening?" Clint asked as he took slow, backward steps. "Or should I just assume you're another glory hound out to make a name for himself?"

But Lantiss wasn't biting. Instead, he simply looked at Clint wearing that smile that made the thick mustache curl on his upper lip like a caterpillar writhing in the heat. The small, triangular goatee on his chin twitched slightly when he finally decided to speak. "You don't get an explanation."

"Then what do you want from me?"

"Drop the gun," Lantiss said simply.

With the pistol pressed against his skull, Clint could see the hammer on Lantiss's weapon was cocked. One wrong twitch and it would all be over.

Out of options for the moment, Clint dropped his Colt.

"Now get on your knees."

Clint's mind raced for a way out. He knew he had seconds to live unless he came up with something in half that time. In an effort to buy some time, he slowly lowered himself down onto his knees.

The smile on Lantiss's face got just a little wider.

THIRTEEN

"Drop the gun, boy," the man with the knife said, his words punctuated by hot, stinking breath against West's neck.

"Who sent you?" West asked while his free hand wrapped around the bigger man's wrist.

The edge of the blade scraped against West's skin, making a grating noise that filled his ears even though it wasn't any louder than the razor that had given him his morning's shave. "You ain't in no position to bargain."

West took in a breath, making sure it wasn't deep enough to push his neck harder against the blade. "Very sloppy," he grunted.

The big man's fist tightened around the handle and brought the knife in close enough to break West's skin. "Yeah. It's sure gonna be."

Suddenly, West swung his right hand in a tight arc that brought the handle of his pistol sailing back until it made sharp contact with the outer edge of the big man's leg. The precisely aimed blow landed right on a nerve that ran down that part of the thigh, sending a jolt of pain so powerful through his attacker's system that it forced the hand holding the knife to loosen up just a little bit.

A little was all West needed.

West dug his fingers in around the big man's wrist, burying his nails in flesh and sinking them in as far as he could. When he heard the grunt of pain come from behind him, the agent pulled the knife away, twisted the joint in the exact opposite direction it was intended to go, and kept up the pressure until the blade slid out from between its owner's fingers and rattled to the floor.

Somehow, West had managed to keep hold of his gun. In fact, when he spun around to face the other man, he felt a tingling sensation running through his fingers and knuckles as though he'd been holding on so tightly to his weapon that he'd cut off the circulation in his hand. That feeling wasn't nearly enough, however, to prevent him from raising the gun as the bigger man started bolting toward him.

The attacker glared at West through the eyes of a wild animal. A savage howl gurgled at the back of his throat as he ran toward West with arms outstretched and both hands grasping desperately for any part of him they could close around.

Knowing he was still the one in control, West let the man run up against the barrel of his gun before pulling the trigger once . . . and then a second time, lifting the crazed killer off his feet each time.

Finally, just before West was about to pull his trigger a third time, he felt the weight of the other man fall completely onto him. The killer drooped forward while letting out a final, rattling breath; every one of his muscles going limp at the same time.

It took most of West's own strength to get the body off of him. Once he was able to push the corpse enough in one direction, however, it landed on the floorboards hard enough to send ripples beneath the planks. Hopping over the body, West landed in front of the overturned table that was still pinning down the second gunman.

"That looks painful," West said when he noticed that the gunman might have had at least one broken leg. "This ought to help a bit." His pistol struck outward and landed squarely on the gunman's jaw, putting the man's lights out with a sickening crack of metal against flesh. After a quick spin around his finger, the pistol landed snugly in its holster.

Not wasting another moment, West turned his attention to where Clint had been. His stomach tightened into a tense knot when he saw his friend kneeling in front of a well-dressed man holding a gun to his head.

West knew better than to simply fire at the man in front of Clint, since even the slightest spasm or reflexive twitch would cause the man's finger to tighten around the trigger. Although he couldn't hear what was being said at the other end of the bar, West knew that Clint's time was running out fast.

That was when he spotted something that put a wild idea into his head. He knew from experience that the more he thought about such ideas, the more impossible they seemed. So to counter that downfall, West threw himself into the moment and allowed his body to act without being hampered by his mind.

West dove to the floor just past where the freshest corpse had landed. His hand flashed out and closed around the handle of the knife. Propping himself up on one knee, he flicked the knife in the air so that he could grab it by the blade.

Since the best bet was that the man in front of Clint was working with all the others, West quickly decided on what was the best thing he could say to grab that one's attention.

"Hey," he shouted. "We got West!"

Although the figure didn't move much, he did take a quick glance over his shoulder in response to those words.

As soon as he saw that, West snapped his hand forward and sent the blade whipping through the air. The blade turned end over end, covering the space between either end of the bar in one and a half rotations.

It flashed toward Lantiss in a quicksilver glimmer, whispering to him as it sailed past his body and buried itself deep into the side of the bar.

His move completed for better or worse, West could only sit and watch to see what would happen next.

Clint and Lantiss had reacted to the words they'd heard in similar ways. For a moment, neither man knew quite what to make of it. Then, their meaning sank in, making the relative silence that had settled upon the saloon that much more potent.

When Lantiss had turned to look at who'd spoken, Clint thought he could make his move. But the man holding the gun turned ever so slightly, without moving the .38 so much as a fraction of an inch. Clint knew the gunman could feel any movement he would make just as easily as he could have seen it, which kept him rooted to his spot.

Suddenly, Lantiss pulled back as though invisible hands were working to prevent the execution. Clint noticed this a split second before he saw the glint of metal flying through the air and heard the sound of a blade cutting its path in space.

The knife landed in the bar inches away from his face, its handle wavering slightly on impact.

Just then, Clint felt the barrel of Lantiss's gun move away from his forehead, which was the only thing he'd been waiting for.

His body burst into a flurry of motion, using speed fueled by the knowledge that he only had one chance to make good on his escape. First, his left hand came up to bat away the .38, his muscles twitching as the gun went off less than a foot away from his brow.

Next, his right hand reached out and plucked the knife from where it had been lodged into the thick oaken timber.

The blade came out smoothly and hissed through the air once again, this time arcing toward Lantiss, who was just now turning his full attention back onto Clint.

The smile was long gone from Lantiss's face as he glanced back at his target. His mind had barely had the opportunity to register the fact that the .38 was no longer in his possession, so his hand was squeezing down on nothing but empty air by the time Clint was on his feet in front of him.

In the blink of an eye, Clint had the blade up to Lantiss's throat and was pressing its edge just hard enough to make a shallow slice into his skin. "Doesn't feel too good to be this close to dying, does it?" Clint said in a low, snarling voice.

Lantiss didn't say a word.

Clint wasn't too disappointed by the other man's silence. It felt good enough to knock him unconscious with a left uppercut, which he'd pulled all the way up from his waist.

FOURTEEN

Clint looked around the saloon, his breath coming in deep gasps and his heart beating like a war drum inside his chest. Surprisingly enough, the entire place hadn't cleared out. Besides himself, West, and the scattered bodies of their attackers, there were still a few people huddled in corners or cowering beneath tables. Once the echoes of gunfire had fully died away, the stragglers started poking their heads out to make sure it was safe to be seen.

"Aw, hell," came a weary voice to Clint's right.

Turning on his heels, Clint saw Rick Hartman slowly rising up from the space he'd been crouching behind the bar.

"Are you hurt?" Clint asked.

Eyes wide and searching the room, Hartman pat himself down and then shook his head. "No. But my saloon sure is. I think you shut me down for at least a week with all this shooting and fighting. What the hell went on here? Who were those men?"

"I can't speak for all of them," West said as he walked up to stand at Clint's side. "But that one that you just knocked out is Gerard Lantiss." Craning his neck to get a closer look at the fallen man, West added, "Or is that *the late* Gerald Lantiss?"

Clint looked down at Lantiss as the tension from the last several minutes began to weigh down on his shoulders like a sack of rocks. "He's not late for anything. I didn't kill him."

"Well, you should have," Hartman said as he leaned over the bar. "For what he's done to my place, I should string him from my rafters. No, wait a minute . . . I should wake him up, beat him up some more, and then—"

"Take it easy, Rick," Clint said. "I think there's been plenty of fighting in here already." Looking down at the unconscious figure, he regarded Lantiss with a calculating sneer. "Besides, it's not like he's actually going to get away with what he tried to pull."

West crouched down next to Lantiss and then looked back up at Clint. "I see great minds really do think alike. How about you give me a hand with this one and we can make sure he wakes up in a manner more befitting someone of his . . . stature."

Shaking his head, Clint bent down on Lantiss's other side so both he and West could take hold of the gunman's arms and drag him toward the saloon's back door.

"Whatever you do to him," Hartman called out before they walked outside, "be sure to make it extra painful."

Clint and West dragged Lantiss all the way to the sheriff's office, pulling him behind them as though he wasn't anything more than a sack of month-old potatoes. They started out going down the side of the street, but then they decided to keep to the boardwalks.

"Wouldn't want to disappoint Rick, now would we?" West said with a devilish smirk.

Shaking his head, but laughing all the same, Clint turned onto the next set of steps leading away from the street. He winced at the sound of Lantiss's head and shoulders bouncing off the wooden edges. Although the boardwalks were more level than the street, the constant patter of planks bumping against the back of Lantiss's skull sounded painful enough to both men. Even so, neither one of them did a thing to make the gunman's journey any easier.

They made it to the sheriff's after a nice, leisurely stroll. Clint dropped off the still-sleeping killer while West waited outside. The only man inside the office was a deputy who looked surprised to have a visitor at this hour.

"That one of them men that was shooting up Rick's Place?" the young lawman asked.

Clint dragged Lantiss all the way across the room and let his leg drop heavily on the floor outside one of the small holding cells in the back. "It sure is. Think he can stay here until he wakes up?"

The deputy walked over to unlock the door and helped Clint toss the gunman onto a rickety bunk. It was at about that time that Lantiss began stirring from his uneasy sleep. His eyes came open right as the barred door slammed shut. He tried to move, but knew immediately that his efforts would only be wasted. The throbbing pain coursing throughout every inch of his body didn't help matters, either.

"I'll come by tomorrow to check on him," Clint said.

"The sheriff will be sorry he missed you. One of the other deputies ran off to fetch him once we got word about what was going on at Rick's."

"He'll probably be busy over there for a while. There's plenty more for him to clean up." Heading for the door, Clint said, "Now if you don't mind, there's a bed with my name written all over it. And after the night I've had, I'm not about to keep it waiting. The sheriff knows where to find me if he needs to. Let him know that I'll be leaving town tomorrow morning after breakfast, though."

"Will do, Mister Adams," the deputy said with a nod. "And thanks for your help."

Clint walked outside to find West leaning against a balcony post. The agent struck a match against the wood grain and touched the flame to a thin cigarette hanging from the side of his mouth.

"Everything go all right in there?" West asked.

Clint nodded. "Sure. Was there a reason you didn't want to go inside?"

After taking a long pull from his cigarette, West held the smoke inside and then let it out in a slow, burning fog. "Not really. I just got tired of dragging that fellow's carcass and thought I'd take a moment of peace before diving back into the mix."

"I take it you're not talking about Varillo or the ones who put Lantiss up to this."

"Afraid not," West said while shaking his head. "You're more than capable to handle that lot on your own. As for me . . . I've got to get back to California. Tonight was a pleasant little diversion compared to what's going on out there."

"Anything else you can tell me about what I've gotten myself into?"

"You know how to get to Perro Rojo?"

"I believe so," Clint replied.

"Then there's not a lot else I can tell you." After taking one more puff of the cigarette, West flicked it down into the muddy gutter. "I really appreciate this, Clint," he said while extending his hand. "I'll owe you big-time for helping me out."

Clint shook the agent's hand. "You're damn right you'll owe me. And don't think that I'll ever forget it."

After that, West turned and started walking down the street in the direction of the train station. Although there wasn't a scheduled arrival until the next morning, the sounds of a steam engine could just be heard drifting through the still night air.

West's silhouette was swallowed up by the darkness. Just before it disappeared entirely, he could be seen raising his hand in a curt, parting wave. Then, as the sound of a single engine got somewhat louder in the distance, West was gone.

That was how it usually went, Clint knew. Although he counted Jeremy West among his most trusted friends, he rarely saw the man more than once or twice every year or two. Now that the agent was gone, Clint wasn't sure when he might see him again.

Turning to walk in the opposite direction, Clint headed for the Lone Star Hotel.

FIFTEEN

It wasn't a long walk back to the hotel, but it was enough of a trip to allow Clint to get his second wind before stepping through the hotel's front door. He half expected to see Lily at the desk, but since she owned the hotel it figured she'd give the late shift to someone else. The chunky, middle-aged man who was at the front desk greeted Clint with an offhanded wave and then got back to the serious business of reading the evening paper. Clint thought about heading for the hotel's restaurant on the off chance that he might be able to persuade the cook to fire up the stove for him, but then changed his mind and went straight for the stairs. He needed all the rest he could get. Even though his body felt charged with energy, he knew it wouldn't take much for him to fall asleep once his back hit the mattress.

Clint unlocked the door to room number six and tossed his hat into the shadows in the general direction of the bed. When he found the lantern with one hand and twisted the knob, a warm orange glow filled the room. After sleeping there for the better part of a month, Clint knew every inch of the room like the back of his hand. That was why, even though he only saw the shape out of the corner of his eye, he knew that it didn't belong.

Reflexively, Clint's hand flashed toward the Colt at his side. His body twisted around on the balls of his feet until he was sighting down the weapon's barrel toward the one shape in the room that hadn't been there when he'd left.

Almost immediately, Clint lowered the gun and allowed his muscles to relax.

"I surrender," Lily said as she held her hands up and allowed the sheet she'd been holding around her to drop away from her body.

The raven-haired hotel owner sat on Clint's bed with her back resting against the headboard. Every smooth, generous curve was caressed by the lantern's flickering light, giving her pale skin an even milkier quality. Her full, rounded breasts swayed gently as she moved forward and crawled to the edge of the bed closest to where Clint was standing.

"Just because you own this hotel that gives you the right to sneak into your guest's rooms?" Clint asked as he removed his gun belt and hung it over the back of a nearby chair.

Lily stuck her bottom lip out like a juicy offering. Kneeling at the edge of the bed, she slid her hands around Clint's neck and pulled him in close. "If you want to lodge a complaint, I can help you with that." Easing her fingers down over his chest, she began working her way back up, popping open his shirt buttons one by one as she added, "But I was kind of hoping you'd be up for something a little more than that."

Ever since he'd gotten back into Labyrinth, Clint had been spending plenty of time with Lily McGearson. Although she'd always had her eye on him when he'd been around town over the last several years, she'd only worked up her courage to talk to him recently. And for many nights since then, she'd been making Clint wish that he'd noticed her a lot sooner. He'd even started staying here in her hotel rather than the Labyrinth House, where he used to stay.

Besides sharing their beds with each other, Clint and Lily had been developing a close friendship. She always seemed to know when he'd want to see her most. In fact, Clint felt as though he shouldn't have been surprised to find her in his room on this particular night.

Lily especially loved to hear about Clint's travels. On the few occasions where she actually got to see him in action, she could barely contain herself until they got to a bed before her hands were tearing away his clothing. She wasn't the first woman Clint had met who got a special kind of thrill from being close to gunmen or killers, but she was one of the few who didn't just have a sick taste for blood.

Lily's aphrodisiac of choice was danger. One time she told him she could taste it on him like some kind of spice. What made her different from those other women was that Clint had acquired a taste for her as well. Her skin reminded him of a sweet, exotic dessert that melted on his tongue and trickled down his throat.

When she got to the top button of Clint's shirt, Lily leaned forward and pulled it off with her teeth. Pulling the shirt open, she looked up at him and whispered, "I heard about what happened at Rick's."

Clint moved his hands over the creamy skin of her shoulders and down the curve of her spine. "I kind of thought you would," he said as the tip of her tongue ran over his bare chest.

Her hands moved fleetingly over his skin, touching him just enough to send tingling waves of pleasure just beneath his flesh. "Were you hurt?" she asked.

"Nothing to brag about."

"Good, because I need you healthy to do everything I had planned for tonight."

Clint thought briefly about how early he had to get up the next morning and all of the travel that lay ahead. He thought about those things for all of about two seconds until such notions were driven out of his head by Lily's fingers unfastening his pants and peeling them down from his hips.

Suddenly, staying awake until sunrise didn't seem like such a bad idea.

SIXTEEN

"Evening, Sheriff," the deputy said as the tall lawman stepped through the front door of his office.

Sweeping his feet off from the top of the biggest desk while trying not to spill any paperwork onto the floor, the deputy flew from the sheriff's chair as though the wood had suddenly caught on fire. He waited to get chewed out by the town's head lawman, but all he got for his minor trespass was stony silence. Rather than push his luck, the deputy hurried around the desk to let the sheriff pass.

"Everything all settled at Rick's Place?" the deputy asked.

The sheriff stopped in his tracks, standing like a statue just over the threshold. He wore a long coat buttoned up against the cool night breeze. His hands were covered with thick, loose riding gloves that made him appear to be more of a scarecrow than a man. Craning his neck slowly from side to side, he nodded, reached behind him, and pushed the door shut.

Becoming uneasy, the deputy gestured toward the holding cells. "Mister Adams brought in one of those men that shot up the place. He said he left plenty of them for you

66

to look after." Taking a step forward, he asked, "Was that true? Did any of the others get hurt?"

"What others?" the sheriff asked in a low, scratchy voice.

Hearing that, the deputy's head flinched back as though he'd been swatted on the nose. "The other two that went to fetch you. Dave and Matt. I . . . I thought they was going to go with you once they told you what was going on at Rick's Place."

Taking another step inside the office, the sheriff looked past the deputy. "Yeah. They're fine," he grumbled. "You don't have to worry about them at all."

The deputy let out a puff of air as a relieved smile came onto his face. "Glad to hear it. Some folks've already been coming through here telling me about all the shooting that was going on. I thought you all might have had a little more trouble than you were counting on."

"Who you got locked up back there?"

"Beats me. Mister Adams dropped him off and headed back to his hotel." Walking back toward Lantiss's cell, the deputy said, "He's pretty banged up. Only just opened his eyes a couple minutes ago. Haven't been able to get a word out of him."

Both sheriff and deputy stood in front of the cell, gazing in at the jailed killer like he was a prized zoo exhibit. Seeing the senior lawman, Lantiss got to his feet and walked forward, wrapping his hands around the cold rusted bars.

"So he didn't say nothin' at all?" the sheriff asked. "Not even to Adams?"

Shrugging, the deputy replied, "Not a word, Sheriff. At least not to me. If he said anything else, Mister Adams didn't mention it."

"Good job."

The deputy couldn't help but feel the pride swelling up inside of his chest. It pushed at the inside of his ribs like a warm air bubble that he'd been trying to inflate ever since he'd gotten the small star pinned to his shirt pocket. It was a bubble that immediately burst the moment he saw that the sheriff wasn't talking to him.

Instead, the lawman was staring into the cell, leveling his gaze at the prisoner cooling his heels inside. And it was that prisoner who beamed with emotion . . . except it wasn't pride.

His eyes narrowed into cold slits, Lantiss tightened his grip around the bars until his knuckles turned white with the effort. His face cracked apart in a wicked, triumphant grin and his chest began to tremble with barely suppressed laughter.

"A very good job, indeed," the sheriff said. Only this time, his voice wasn't deep or scratchy. It also most certainly wasn't the sheriff's.

Even though he could barely get himself to believe what was happening, the deputy knew that things were just about to go from strange to worse. Wheeling around to look at the sheriff, he instinctively went for his gun when he saw the pistol coming up to bear on him.

The deputy's biggest mistake was taking one last look at the sheriff's face. Upon closer inspection, he could see several little things about the older lawman that looked out of place. A wrinkle where it shouldn't have been or a mole that had suddenly gone missing. But spotting those things took time, which was all the sheriff needed to press his gun against the deputy's chest and pull the trigger.

Most of the explosion was buffered by the deputy's body. His flesh soaked in the gun's sound and was torn apart by the lead that was spit out of the barrel. The bullet's impact lifted him up to his toes and jerked him back like a muffled sneeze. A spot on his back just below the left shoulder blade burst open as the twisted chunk of lead came tearing through amid a crimson spray.

Just to be sure, the sheriff twisted his wrist to get a

different angle and pulled the trigger again. This time, the body in front of him barely moved. There was just another muffled cough and another splatter of tissue and fluid on the wall.

Pushing the deputy away with his left hand, the sheriff was already heading for the key ring that hung on the wall near the big desk by the time the body slammed to the floor. After plucking the ring from its spot, he tossed the keys across the room where they landed in Lantiss's waiting hand.

Lantiss made quick work out of finding the right key. Once the lock snapped and the door swung open, he hurried out and tossed the keys back to the sheriff. "You want to give me a hand?" he asked.

Between the both of them, they got the deputy's body stuffed into the cell in less than a minute or two. Lantiss shut the cell door with a triumphant flourish of his hand.

The sheriff took the keys and hung them back in place, stepping to the window so he could take a look outside from the edge of the window. "I don't think anyone heard the shots," he said after carefully scanning the street. "Now get out of here and head for the meet-up point before you miss the fireworks."

"Can you get out all right on your own?"

Reaching up to his face, the sheriff grabbed the end of his nose, twisted, and pulled out the skin like so much taffy. The rubbery substance extended for a few inches before tearing free, exposing another smaller nose beneath the flesh-colored shell.

"I'll be fine," he said from behind the shredded second face.

SEVENTEEN

Lily's mouth worked over Clint's body, exploring every inch of him as though she wanted to taste him from head to toe. Her tongue flicked out here and there, teasing his most sensitive areas until he started to moan her name softly and writhe beneath her hips.

Straddling his waist, Lily raised up so that the ends of her hair dragged along his chest as her nails scraped gently along his sides. The only thing she wore was a thin black choker that was made of soft velvet. When she straightened all the way up, Lily arched her back and pushed her breasts out proudly.

Much to Clint's pleasure, she had an awful lot to be proud of. Every one of her curves were smooth and flowing. Her large breasts swung heavily above his lips as she leaned forward and touched one hard nipple onto his lips just enough for him to feel the smooth skin. When he tried to take her into his mouth, Clint heard her giggle mischievously before she pulled away.

"Not yet," she said softly.

His penis was hard as stone and pressed against the warm dampness between her legs. Expertly moving her hips up and down, Lily stroked his shaft between the lips of her vagina in a similar way that her mouth brushed over the rest of his body.

The motion was enough to turn Clint's breaths into shallow gasps. His hands reached out and closed around her breasts, squeezing her hard nipples between his fingertips.

Now it was Lily's turn to gasp as she clenched her teeth and squeezed her eyes shut as the sensations coursed through her flesh. Her legs clamped shut tightly around him, holding Clint firmly in place. Keeping her eyes closed, she leaned her head back and lifted herself up, allowing Clint to guide himself inside of her.

Pushing up with his hips while Lily came down, Clint buried his cock deep between her legs, thrusting into her hot depths, causing both of them to cry out in shared pleasure. Clint kept his hands on her body, savoring the way she moved on top of him. He tried taking his hands away from her breasts, but Lily grabbed hold of his wrists with insistent strength, forcing him to keep touching her in just the right spot.

Not one to disappoint a lady, Clint kneaded her breasts and rubbed her nipples over the palm of his hands. She especially loved it when he traced his thumbs down the center of her cleavage while cupping her in his grasp.

"Oh, Clint," she moaned. "You feel so good."

Clint didn't know if she was talking about his hands roaming down her body or his cock pumping steadily in and out of her. Not that it mattered, however, since he wasn't planning on stopping either anytime soon.

Shifting beneath her writhing form, Clint moved so that he was sitting up with Lily facing him on his lap. He was still inside of her when he enclosed her in both of his arms and started kissing her passionately on the mouth. Their tongues darted between each other's lips, tasting one another while Clint slowly pushed himself deeper inside of her.

Lily brought her legs up so she could wrap them around

Clint's waist. Purposely disengaging from him, she
crawled back onto his lap and shook the coal-black hair
from her face. "You know why I came here tonight?" she
asked while nibbling his ear.

Reaching down, Clint rubbed her glistening clit until he
could hear Lily's breath catch in the back of her throat.
"Was it to feel this?"

With him drawing slow, tiny circles around the delicate
nub of flesh between her thighs, Lily was unable to say
another word until Clint moved his hands to the inside of
her legs. Finally, after pulling some air into her lungs, she
said, "I heard about how you dealt with those killers and
I felt like I was right there beside you.

"I could almost see your muscles flexing," she purred
while rubbing his shoulders and arms. "When I closed my
eyes . . . I swore I could hear your heart pounding in your
chest. Just like it is right now."

As she spoke, Lily's entire body responded to what she
was saying. The sides of her mouth curled up into a wistful
smile. Her head and torso swayed from side to side like a
reed being nudged by a passing breeze. Even the muscles
inside her legs clenched around him as though she was
hanging on for dear life.

"I'll tell you something," Clint said as he moved his
hands over her hips to clasp at the small of her back. "My
heart feels like it's beating faster now than it ever was in
any saloon fight."

Lily's eyes snapped open and her smile turned into a
broad grin. "Really? Then maybe I was there with you . . .
in spirit."

"You were in a way," Clint replied. "Because when all
that shooting started, there was a little part of me that was
thinking what a charge you'd get out of it all."

"Oh, Clint. That's so sweet."

"No, it's strange."

"Maybe . . . but in a sweet kind of way."

For a second, they simply looked across at one another, staring deeply into each other's eyes. Clint felt as though he was starting to fall forward, toppling through space even though he was simply leaning forward to kiss Lily gently on the lips. She met him halfway, nibbling on his lips while sucking gently.

The kiss became more passionate and soon Clint's body was aching to be inside of hers. He knew she was feeling the same thing by the way Lily started moaning softly and pressing herself against him. Finally, she reached down to hold his penis in both hands while caressing the shaft gently between her palms.

Clint returned the favor by slipping his fingers over the edge of her pussy lips, rubbing the slick, silky skin up and down before easing them slowly inside. Their lips pulled apart so that both of them could lean back and watch the other's face while their hands continued the intimate massage.

Just when Clint thought he wouldn't be able to take any more, he moved back and gently pushed Lily onto her back. She reached up and put her fingers to her mouth while arching her back like a content cat. Knowing what he wanted to do, she spread her legs and held her breath, waiting to feel Clint's mouth between her legs.

Running his hands along the outside of her thighs, Clint lowered his face down to her wet pussy and started placing little kisses along the upper edge of the dark thatch of hair between her legs. Using only the tip of his tongue, he teased her clit and then took a long, lingering taste of her. Lily thrust her hips up into his face while moaning loudly as Clint's tongue went to work on her.

By the time he allowed himself to bury his face between her thighs, Clint had to hold on tightly to Lily's hips before she bucked out from underneath him. He could feel the orgasm sweeping through her as Lily's muscles started tensing beneath her flesh. She moaned louder and louder until her voice was echoing through the room and her hips were pressed tightly against his face.

Sweating with exertion, Lily dropped back down onto the bed and pulled reluctantly away from Clint's mouth. "I need you inside of me," she groaned.

Clint positioned himself over Lily's body, his rigid cock aching to penetrate her. As soon as he lowered himself on top of her, Clint could feel Lily's hand stroking him, guiding him into her waiting vagina.

Once he was inside of her, Clint thrust his hips forward and drove himself deep inside, slamming against her just hard enough to bring another grunt of pleasure from the back of Lily's throat. Holding her hands tightly over her head, Clint pounded into her while staring into her wide, excited eyes.

Lily wriggled beneath him, her hands pinned to the mattress over her head as her body was ravaged toward a second explosion of pleasure. She spread her legs open wider, tossing her head back deeper into the pillow as Clint pounded into her again and again until he drove in one final time, his own orgasm running rampant through his entire body.

When he was finally able to move again, Clint released Lily's hands so she could gently scratch his back. It felt good to stay entwined with her and she didn't seem at all anxious for him to move.

"Oh, Clint," she whispered after a few minutes had passed in blissful silence. "That was . . . that was . . ."

"I know," he said. "Me, too."

It wasn't much, but that was all that needed to be said at that moment. Before long, Clint and Lily were wrapped in each other's arms beneath soft layers of sheets and blankets, the entire room bathed in cool darkness.

The furthest thing from Clint's mind was the fight at the saloon or the mission that lay ahead. For those moments, with Lily snuggled up against him, all he could think about was the smell of her hair so close to his face and the smooth texture of her skin against his.

Everything was perfect just then.

That was Lily's gift to him.

A calm before the storm.

EIGHTEEN

Morning came and went as it always did at the start of any day. When Clint awoke, he found himself lying next to a woman who seemed all the more beautiful after being rumpled from the previous night's sleep and other activities. Lily stirred the moment he crawled out of bed, opening her eyes as soon as his feet hit the cool wood floor.

"Are you really leaving so soon?" she asked.

Clint slipped into his clothes. The more he thought about where he was headed and what he was going to do, the more uncomfortable he felt without his Colt strapped around his waist. "Afraid so," he said while buckling the gun belt.

"Where're you headed?"

Clint's first impulse was to answer her question straight away. Then, he remembered who he was working for and thought better of the idea. "South," was all he decided to tell her.

Propping herself up on one elbow, Lily regarded him with a somewhat amused expression. "Can you at least tell me when you might be back?"

"No," Clint said in all honesty. "And I'd appreciate it if you forgot I even told you as much as I did."

Lily sat up with her back against the headboard. Gathering the sheets up to cover her, she ran her fingers through her hair until it flowed evenly over her shoulders. "It's all right if you don't want to tell me. I don't expect you to treat me like anything more than I am. I figured it would be this way when I came to your room that first time."

Clint let out a heavy sigh and turned away from the window. Even though he knew she wasn't as hurt as she was letting on, the tone in her voice and the pout on her lips were still enough to strike all the right chords inside of him.

"First of all," he said while sitting on the bed next to her, "I happen to be very fond of what we've got. It may not be what you might call traditional, but it sure seems to work for both of us. Also, we might not have known each other our whole lives, but you know me well enough that you shouldn't be surprised when I pick up and leave town."

Reaching out to run his fingers beneath her chin, Clint drew her toward him until he could brush his lips against hers. "The one thing I can tell you for certain is that I will be back."

And before she could say another word, Lily was silenced by a gentle kiss that quickly grew in passion until they were both close to losing themselves completely in the moment. Finally, Clint forced himself to break away from her and step toward the door.

"Trust me, Lily," he said. "If I had my choice, I'd much rather stay here with you than head out to where I'm going."

"Then why not stay? If . . . whatever this is . . . is so dangerous, why not just forget about it and stay here? It's not like the world will just shrivel up and die without the great Clint Adams riding from one corner of it to another. If you ask me, I'd say you'd be doing a lot of people a big favor if you tried a little harder to keep yourself alive."

"That's funny. I always thought you liked seeing me risk my neck."

Lily's skin turned a deep shade of pink while she turned her eyes away from Clint's. "Maybe I do," she said. "But that's only because you make me feel so . . . safe. Knowing what I know about you, I feel like you're the only man alive who's worth trusting. The only one who can protect me against anything or anyone out there."

Smiling, Clint walked back to the bedside. "And all this time I just figured you had a thing for my gun."

This time, it was Lily who reached out. For a moment, it looked as though she was extending her hand toward Clint's crotch. Then, at the last second, she moved her hand so she could brush her fingertips along the top of his Colt. Looking up at him, she winked and said, "Well, maybe there's a little of that in me, too."

With that, the mood in the room brightened up just as much as the early morning sky outside Clint's window. They laughed and made small talk while Clint prepared himself for his ride to Perro Rojo. Although she didn't ask about what he was preparing to do, Lily also didn't treat his leaving as some taboo subject. Instead, she simply enjoyed the time they had together as they ate breakfast and packed up his clothes.

More than anything, Clint wanted to tell her all about the mission involving Diego Varillo and the Ghost Squadron. Part of him simply wanted to share the story with someone else, while the other part screamed at him not to. He knew which part had to be obeyed and held his tongue.

Once Clint climbed onto Eclipse's back, he took up the reins and looked down at Lily's face. She gave him one last kiss and waved good-bye. There was something about the look in her eyes that bothered Clint. It was something disturbing, yet all too familiar.

It wasn't that she was obviously going to miss him.

It was that she seemed to think she would never see him again.

Rather than let that thought haunt him all they way to Mexico, Clint did his best to put it out of his mind and ride on. After all . . . there was nothing else for him to do.

NINETEEN

Although Clint had heard of the town called Perro Rojo, that didn't mean the little border settlement was easy to find. The ride south toward the border took the better part of three days. Since there wasn't much in West Texas besides wide-open spaces and the occasional lawless haven for dregs and murderers, Clint didn't waste his time stopping in any of the rugged towns he came across along the way.

Being recognized in one of those places would have led to a fight. There was no two ways about it. In towns that were too small or too rough to bother with law, the only way for a man to get ahead was to best someone higher up on the food chain. Clint didn't have time to take part in anything like that, so he kept the stars over his head and the ground against his back.

What he lost in comfort was more than made up for in the time he saved. As for Eclipse, the Darley Arabian seemed more than happy to remain in the open air after being cooped up in a stable for the last couple of weeks. As opposed to his rider, the stallion kept his head high and his steps lively. If it was possible, Clint swore he would have seen Eclipse smile.

The sun hung overhead like a ball of flame that had melted onto the roof of the world. It blazed down from overhead, baking everything below from the skin on Clint's back to the ground beneath his feet. After the third day of travel, even Eclipse was beginning to slow down. But the stallion struggled to keep up his pace, even with the flies chewing at his flanks and the sand blowing in his eyes.

Taking off his hat, Clint wiped his brow with the back of his hand and fanned himself in an attempt to drive away some of the oppressive heat. "I don't know about you," he said to the back of Eclipse's head, "but I'm about ready to head for the next town I see . . . no matter how big of a hole in the ground it is."

Eclipse responded to the sound of Clint's voice by bobbing his head and putting a little more strength behind his plodding hooves.

Clint set the hat back on top of his head and straightened up in the saddle. Shading his eyes, he scanned the horizon and took a mental bearing of his position.

"The way I see it, we should be about another half day's ride or so away from the border. I know Perro Rojo's around here somewhere, but I don't know exactly where."

Eclipse huffed and shook his head as a swarm of gnats buzzed around his eyes and ears.

After the last couple of days with the Darley Arabian as his only companion, this was the closest thing to a conversation he could expect. Once the stallion had stopped shaking and fidgeting with the flying insects, Clint reached out to scratch Eclipse's bristly mane.

"I know I've never been to this town," he said to himself as much as the horse. "But that doesn't mean I won't find it. Besides, this Lieutenant Muller will wait for me if I'm a little late. He'd better, anyway."

It was at about that time that Clint realized two things.

First: He was about to continue a prolonged discussion with the back of Eclipse's head.

Second: He needed to take a break and spend some time around other human beings. Any human beings.

Less than an hour later, like an answer to his unspoken request, the vague outline of a group of buildings could be seen in the distance. Clint didn't bother with the spyglass in his saddlebag. Instead, he simply pointed Eclipse toward the structures and kept riding.

It didn't take long for Clint to reach the buildings he'd spotted. This was partly due to the fact that time seemed to roll by a little faster when there was nothing to see or hear but ground passing by and the clomp of hooves on packed soil. Also, the town simply wasn't as far away as Clint had thought after first spotting it. It was an easy mistake to make since there were only half a dozen buildings making up the place and four of those looked as though they'd been kicked over by a passing giant.

Only one roof was whole, leaving the rest in various states of disrepair ranging from holes the size of Clint's torso to half of the top floor being exposed to the sun's baking rays. The walls looked a little better, but not by much. As he was passing by some of them, Clint started to wonder if a passing cannon brigade had set up and taken potshots at the town not too long ago.

But that seemed unlikely since the holes were too big to have been left by a cannon. Also, cannon holes were generally neater than the jagged chasms displayed on these structures like so many festering sores on a rotting corpse.

Clint kept riding down the middle of the two short rows of leaning structures, wondering if he hadn't simply come across a ghost town. For a ghost town, the place wasn't all that bad. Actually, it seemed about right. But then he started seeing people sticking their heads out from empty windowpanes or stepping out from one of the bigger sections of missing wall.

For the most part, surprise was the predominant expression on the faces Clint saw. Suspicious hostility was a close second.

Clint turned in the saddle to tip his hat to one of the locals before he ducked back into what little shelter he could get in one of the buildings. When he turned back to look at where he was going, he had to pull back quickly on the reins before Eclipse walked straight out of town.

Hopping down to stretch his legs, Clint led the stallion to what he thought was either a water trough or a small, oblong crate that was missing its lid. "Excuse me," he said to one of the figures huddling in the shadows. "Is there anyplace I can go for a drink or maybe some food?"

He didn't get an answer.

"All I want is—" Clint stopped himself in mid-sentence when his eyes caught a glimpse of a wide plank of wood sticking out of the ground. On one end of the chunk of lumber was a couple fragmented words scrawled in fading white paint.

WE   OME T   PER O R JO.

TWENTY

It had taken some work on his part, but Lantiss was finally able to convince Rebecca Chase to accompany him on the ride to the border. Although the woman accepted the fact that she was with him as long as he could take her to Varillo, she wasn't at all happy about making the long trip to Mexico on horseback rather than the comfort of a stage.

Her only consolation was the fact that she'd been able to make him regret bringing her along during every step of the way.

Dressed in battered jeans and a thick cotton shirt, Rebecca looked like the polar opposite of the woman she was when working the crowds at saloons and gambling halls. In fact, the material hung so loosely around her that it all but covered up the supple curves of her body, another fact that she absolutely despised.

"I still don't see why I had to travel with *you*," she said, spitting out the last word as though it tasted bad. "Diego would have sent a coach for me sooner or later."

Lantiss shook his head, a part of him longing for the quiet solitude of his cell back in Labyrinth. "There is no more 'later'. Either you came with me now, or you would have stayed behind."

"Well, I would've been better off in Labyrinth. At least there I could sleep in a real bed and eat hot food."

"You'll have all the hot food you can stomach once we cross over into Mexico. Until then, just do me a favor and shut the hell up."

Rebecca pouted for a second, but stopped once she was certain that Lantiss wasn't watching her. Then, bringing her horse up alongside the other man's, she tried a different tack. "We don't have to fight like this, you know. I can be very easy to get along with once you get to know me."

"Yeah . . . I heard that much about you. Well, the easy part, anyway."

"You're one to talk," she sneered as her voice suddenly took on a sharper quality. "It wasn't me who wound up sitting in jail the night before we were supposed to leave. What's the matter? Was that the only way you could think of to mess this whole thing up?"

"I got out of prison just fine . . . no thanks to you."

Rebecca sat back in her saddle and nodded. "That's right. Another one of Diego's men had to come rescue you. What do you think the colonel will say once he finds out about that? You think he'll still consider you worth the money he's paying?"

Lantiss pulled back on his reins, bringing his mount to a sudden stop. Taking a moment to draw a deep breath, he twisted in his saddle to grab Rebecca by the front of her shirt. "Listen up, bitch," he snarled. "You may be one of Colonel Varillo's favorite spies, but to me you ain't nothing but a damn insect chewing its way beneath my skin.

"Take a look around you," he said while physically moving her back and forth with so much force he nearly tossed her off her horse. "Do you see Varillo or anyone else around here who favors you so much?"

When she didn't answer, Rebecca saw the burning anger

in Lantiss's eyes. Steeling herself against him, she said,
". . . No."

"That's right," Lantiss raged. "You're out in the middle
of nowhere with a man who kills women and children for
a living. So since you fit right in one of those categories,
I'd suggest you use the brain that God gave you and shut
your fucking hole before I drill another one through the
middle of your skull."

The next few moments passed in tense silence.

When it was clear that neither one of the riders was
about to say another word, Lantiss shoved Rebecca away
and let go of her shirt. Without checking to see if she
would follow him, he turned his horse toward the southern
horizon and snapped the reins.

Letting him get thirty or forty feet in front of her, Rebecca straightened her clothes and touched her heels to the
sides of her mare. The only thing keeping her from doing
anything else was the fact that she knew damn well that
Lantiss was telling the truth about why he'd been hired by
Varillo. In fact, she'd heard about jobs that the killer had
taken that would make most butchers turn away in disgust.
And there were always plenty of jobs that nobody knew
about.

One of the things that made her feel better, however,
was the fact that Lantiss only knew a fraction of what she
did to survive in Varillo's company. For the moment, that
was exactly the way she liked it. Rebecca knew how to
bow her head and look frightened by all the men as they
postured and screamed like animals. In fact, she was an
expert in using their own apelike responses as a means to
get her own ends.

Whether her weapon was her pistol or her body, Rebecca knew just where to strike and exactly when to make
the killing blow. She watched Lantiss ride on ahead, making sure not to allow her own horse to get to close to him.
And when . . . not if . . . he looked over his shoulder at her,

Rebecca would be wearing the perfect mask of respect laced with fear.

And he would eat it up just like she was offering him crumbs from the palm of her hand.

The minutes dragged by.

Then they turned into hours.

Finally, after waiting and watching for no less than four hours, Rebecca caught Lantiss slowing his pace and taking a furtive look over his shoulder.

He looked at her for only a second before turning back around. Anther couple seconds later, he pulled back on his reins and allowed Rebecca to catch up to him.

"Here," he said while offering his canteen in extended hand. "You'd best take a drink of this before you fall over. I wouldn't want you hurt before you got to Colonel Varillo."

Rebecca slowly raised her head, flinching slightly when he pushed the canteen toward her. Taking it in slightly trembling hands, she lifted it to her lips and took a long drink. Some of the water trickled down her chin and ran between her breasts to mingle with the grit and sweat that stuck the cotton shirt to her body like a second skin.

"Thank you so much," she said timidly.

Lantiss snatched the canteen from her hands and slung it back across his saddle horn. "Just try and keep up. We're nearly there. And . . . if you need another drink . . . let me know."

After a meek nod, Rebecca averted her eyes and let the killer ride on ahead. She watched with interest as his back straightened and his chin lifted up high as though he was some kind of hero for dominating an unarmed woman.

The very notion was nearly enough to force a smile onto Rebecca's face. As long as she knew how to speak just the right way, turn her hips properly, and allow enough of her body to be put on display, she knew she would always have a weapon against any man.

TWENTY-ONE

Clint saw his current situation as a good as well as bad thing. The good part was that he didn't have to ride anymore under the blazing sun with nothing more to occupy his mind than how long the next crack in the soil would be. The bad part was that, as a stranger riding through the middle of a town that was only six buildings, he might as well have announced his presence with a fireworks display.

Not exactly the best way to represent a division of the government with the word *secret* in its title.

Trying to make the best out of a potentially lethal situation, Clint hoped that Varillo's men weren't looking for a candidate for target practice and slapped on the best clueless grin he could manage. All things considered, that part wasn't difficult at all.

"Uhhh, excuse me again," he said to the figure who was still watching him from inside the closest dilapidated building. "I could really use some food."

Clint must have done a good job of looking helpless, harmless, or both because the figure in the shadows came a little closer toward the light. It looked as though whoever it was had been stooped over to avoid getting hit in the head by low-hanging beams. Then, at second glance, Clint could see that the figure wasn't hunched over at all. Instead, it was naturally a little closer to the ground than normal.

Although his face bore the scars and lines of someone in their late thirties or even early forties, the man's body was about the size of a small child's. Wearing a dented bowler on his head and a vest over a dirty, yellowed shirt, the stout little man waddled toward Clint with a crooked frown on his face.

"Use yer eyes, mister," said the little man. "If you got an ounce of sense, you'd move on to someplace that cares if you starve to death or not."

The little man might have been a somewhat comical sight if not for the expression on his face. He glared up at Clint as though he was about to spit. The little, rust-colored teeth in his mouth were bared.

"I don't think I caught your name," Clint said.

Dropping down so that he sat with his back against the wall, the little man took hold of a stick and drew idle circles in the sand. "That's because I didn't give it," he grunted.

Clint reached inside his pocket and removed a couple of folded dollar bills. "Look, if it's too much trouble to ask for directions around here, then I can just as easily go somewhere that knows how to treat visitors."

"Visitors?" the little man said as his eyes locked onto the cash Clint was holding. His entire face lit up as though the sun had only then found a path through the cracked plaster. "I didn't know we had comp'ny. That's altogether different."

In a flash, the little man was on his feet and snatching the money Clint was offering. The motion was so fluid that it made Clint wonder if the strange little guy wouldn't have been able to get the bills even if he hadn't bent down to him.

Weighing the money in rounded fingers, the squat little

man stuffed it into his pants pocket and clasped his hands over his stomach. "Name's Juan. We ain't got much in Perro Rojo, but if it's here, I know where it's at." Rising up to his tiptoes, Juan added, "And you might be surprised to know just how much comes through this place."

Clint's expression was light, yet cast in stone. He didn't so much as twitch at Juan's offer for information. "Actually . . . a drink's all I need for now, thanks."

Juan ran his fingers through the thinning, greasy hair that swirled on top of his head. Squinting up through the dust and sun, he studied Clint for a good amount of time before waving toward one of the smallest, most run-down shacks. "You can drink yer fill in there. But it won't be hardly worth what you paid to get there."

Offhandedly, Clint said, "Then I'll expect you to be ready to make good on the rest of that payment I gave you."

Juan lowered his head and slumped back as though he'd already fallen asleep. "I'll be right here. Ain't nowhere to go in this damn place than right here."

If the midget said anything else, Clint wasn't paying close enough attention to catch it. Instead, he was more preoccupied by the street that separated him from the shack that Juan had pointed out. Even though there did seem to be more activity going on in that particular structure, that wasn't what was foremost on Clint's mind right that second.

What bothered him more were the four men who seemed to have appeared out of nowhere and were walking straight toward him. Walking in two rows, the men took up the entire street and judging by the intense looks on their faces, they were anything but the town's welcoming committee.

Rather than give the group any more time to collect their thoughts, Clint swung down from the saddle, turned to face them head-on, and started walking right for them.

The members of the group were all dressed in shredded rags without a single buckle between them. One of them had half a pair of suspenders holding up his britches while the other three had rope tied around their waists. They appeared to be Mexicans, but when they got a little closer, it was hard to tell whether the color of their skin was an effect of the sun, their heritage, or the layers of dirt caked onto their flesh.

Clint planted his feet and let his arm hang down near his Colt. Looking into the approaching men's eyes, Clint saw nothing but bad intentions. They stared back at him the way a bobcat might study a wounded prairie dog, their faces reflecting the cruel simplicity of their intent.

They came to a stop about ten feet in front of him. The man with the broken suspenders tilted his head and curled his lips back in a distasteful sneer.

"You walk into the wrong place, gringo," he said.

TWENTY-TWO

Clint stood without moving a muscle. He was ready for whatever the four men wanted to throw at him, but wasn't about to make the first move. Years of finding himself in these kinds of situations had given him the experience to know how to handle himself around this type of animal.

No sudden moves.

Show no fear.

Be ready.

What concerned him the most was that he couldn't quite make out what the two men in the back were doing. Knowing whether or not they already had their guns drawn might just make all the difference in how this turned out. And at times like these, that difference was between life and death.

Clint stared into the eyes of the man with the suspenders, gambling that he was the one leading this group.

"You fellas have a problem with visitors?" Clint asked. "Maybe you should've posted a sign."

"We'll post a sign over yer grave. That should be plenty to scare the rest away."

Reaching out with all his senses, Clint was suddenly aware that there was someone coming up behind him.

Whoever it was did a good job of trying to remain unnoticed, but Clint's instincts were just too sharp to let something like that slip by. Before he could do anything about it, however, he heard the footsteps come to a stop and a harsh, scratchy voice sound from over his left shoulder.

"All the man wants is a drink," the voice said. "Wouldn't it be easier to let him have one than go through all this fuss?"

Clint didn't want to take his eyes away from the four locals, so he took a few cautious steps to one side. When his back touched against the side of the closest building, he got a look at the newest arrival out of the corner of his eye.

The man stood a little shorter than him, but was wider through the shoulders. His face was covered with a thick beard and long strands of light brown hair poured down from beneath a battered hat. Acknowledging Clint with a curt nod, the man once again turned his attention to the four locals.

"Now even though you still outnumber us two to one," he said, "something still tells me that you won't be doing anything else right now besides turning around and walking away."

The one in suspenders shifted his eyes between Clint and the man next to him, regarding each in turn with a cold, measuring stare. "Two-to-one odds . . . they seem pretty good to me. But four-to-one seems a lot better."

For a moment, Clint wasn't sure what the local was talking about. Then, the man wearing the suspenders lifted his head and looked to either side as a yellow-stained smile appeared beneath his greasy mustache.

Clint took a quick look up, making sure to keep the four men in his peripheral vision. When he glanced to where the other man had indicated, Clint saw several other faces looking down at him from the tops of the nearby buildings. Some poked their faces out of broken windows or the ruins of what had once been second floors, while others sat on flat rooftops with their legs dangling over the sides.

If the man with the suspenders could be criticized about anything, it wasn't his math skills. Of the people watching them from above, four of them were brandishing anything from rifles to shotguns. At least, that was as many as Clint could see with his one quick glance.

"Let me guess," the stocky man next to Clint said under his breath. "More of them up on the rooftops, right?"

"Yeah," Clint said, making sure he had a solid wall to his back. "I saw three across the street and another one on our side."

"Sounds about right."

"I take it you know these guys?"

"Well enough to know what's going through their minds."

The locals crept in closer around them like a hand slowly tightening around an exposed throat. As far as Clint could tell, the ones on the rooftops were already prepared to fire. It seemed as though they were only waiting for a signal from their leader. Thinking along those lines, Clint's eyes went back to the man in suspenders. He knew that trying to talk to them was pointless, which didn't leave him with a whole lot of alternatives.

"Get ready to move," the man next to Clint whispered.

Before he could do another thing, Clint saw a flicker of movement come from the stout figure at his side. From that point on, he acted purely on instinct as everything else in the world seemed to slow down around him.

A shot blasted through the air next to Clint, but didn't take down any of the four men standing in front of them. Instead, the stout figure was aiming for the rooftops and had managed to pick off one of the riflemen who'd taken up a spot there.

Following the other man's lead once he saw that the locals at street level weren't about to move right away,

Clint drew and squeezed off a shot in one fluid motion. His body had been preparing for the action ever since he looked into the locals' eyes and now that he followed through, Clint felt like an arrow that had finally been allowed to fly.

His upper body twisted to face the sniper who had the most direct line of sight to him while his arm went through its motions so fast that it was nothing more than a blur sprouting from his body. The Colt bucked once against his palm and the rifleman on the nearby roof lurched back and fell out of sight.

Before taking another shot, Clint turned back to see what the original four were doing. He got ready to throw himself down to the ground or into the building behind him if necessary, but soon realized that he might not have to do either one just yet.

The stout figure at Clint's side stood with his gun held in a relaxed hand. He kept his body loose so that he was ready to defend himself or take another shot at any one of the local gunmen if the situation arose. "I'd say that evened things up a bit," he said with a slight grin. "Care for us to whittle down the odds a little more?"

Clint kept his mouth shut for the moment, watching to see how the locals would react to what they'd just seen and heard. The man in suspenders fidgeted on his feet, almost as though he was of two minds on whether he should draw or run. Finally, with his hand perched within an inch of his holster, he made his decision.

"You have your drink," the man said grudgingly. "But make it quick."

With that, the man in suspenders held up one hand and called off the dogs around him. The three others in the street seemed only too glad to step back and head for the shelter of a crooked doorway. As for the ones sitting on the rooftops, they moved back and disappeared. Every one of the windows had also suddenly become vacant.

Keeping his pistol in hand, Clint turned to get his first good look at the man who'd stepped up beside him. Now that he could make out more than sketchy details of the figure, he noticed that the stout man looked every bit as weathered as the buildings around him. His skin was cracked and pitted with scars of every size and shape, but looked as though it could take the heat of a fire without so much as a twitch.

His clothes hung off him as if they'd been buttoned around a tree trunk. Beneath a long coat were a pair of gun belts crisscrossing at the waist, the casings of several spare bullets glinting in the fading light. Oddly enough, the last thing to catch Clint's attention was the man's most distinguishing characteristic: His right leg stopped short just below the knee, where it was replaced by a gnarled wooden brace, which tapered down to a stump slightly thicker than the leg of a chair.

"So what do you say?" the man asked. "Still up for that drink?"

TWENTY-THREE

The inside of what Perro Rojo called a saloon looked as though it had already been through the worst any structure could ever hope for. The surface of the walls were blackened and obviously scorched by fire, although it was impossible to tell whether the saloon had caught ablaze or if it had simply been pieced together from other buildings that had. Either way, the air stank of ash as well as the pungent odors of too many people crammed into too small of a space.

Instead of anything resembling a bar, there were only a stack of old crates piled about four feet high. Behind that, an old woman shuffled back and forth filling glasses from bottles that might very well have been pulled from the bottom of a river.

The ceiling over Clint's head was swarming with moths and their bodies crunched beneath his boots as he followed the squat man toward a pair of chairs near the back of the room. Making sure to keep his back to the wall and his eyes facing the door, Clint took a seat. He regretted it instantly when something he could only hope was water soaked in through the bottom of his jeans and back of his legs.

Once they were both seated, Clint looked around the room for any of the faces he'd seen outside. As far as he could tell, there weren't any of the gunmen in the crowd. More than that, nobody in the place seemed to give a damn that they were there at all.

The one-legged man motioned toward the old lady and then held up two fingers. Once the order was placed, he looked over at Clint. "So you're Adams?"

"That's right."

"Good. I'd hate to think I tossed my fat into the fire just for some stranger who wandered into this hole of a town by mistake."

Clint shook his head slightly. The word *mistake* echoed in his brain like a bad omen. "Then that would make you Mister Muller."

The man turned his weather-beaten face until he could lock his eyes onto Clint's. "*Lieutenant* Muller," he corrected. "And yes . . . that would be me."

Satisfied, Clint allowed himself to ease back into the warped chair. Since he was already stained by the filthy wood, he might as well make himself comfortable. "Does this place always greet newcomers that way, or am I something special?"

Muller used the little finger of his left hand to dig at something stuck between his teeth. "You got that right," he said once he'd found what he'd been looking for and flicked it to the ground. "And don't feel too bad about your little reception. This ain't exactly what you'd call a hub of good manners."

The sound of hustling, shuffling feet was soon followed up by the slam of two glasses onto the little end table between Clint and Muller. Brown liquid inside the glasses was probably whiskey, but it could have also been any number of things that had been stained to its current color.

Muller put some coins into the woman's steady hand and reached for his glass. "Drink up," he said. "If the folks around here know anything, it's their liquor. I guess that just comes naturally when you spend your days living in a heap of burnt timber."

Picking up his glass, Clint raised it to his nose and took a whiff. The scent alone nearly singed the hair inside his nostrils and sent a heat wave all the way through his sinuses to settle in the pit of his stomach. As for what it was . . . that part was still anyone's guess. "I appreciate the drink," he said, "but I think I'll have to pass."

"I'd advise strongly against asking for water. It's darker than what you got in front of ya. And unless you don't mind chewing your beer, I'd have to steer you away from that as well."

"Then how about we skip the drinks and get right to the reason I'm in this place. From what I've been told, we shouldn't be wasting our time sitting around any saloon discussing the local spirits."

"You sure got that right," Muller said. Lifting the glass to his lips, he tossed back the potent concoction and swallowed with a grimace. He clenched his teeth and dropped the empty glass onto the table while letting out a hiss that sounded like it had come from a steam engine. "That little greeting party you ran into wasn't just a group of locals with their dander up. They belong to Varillo . . . every last one of 'em . . . and they're here to guard this town against anyone who might stick his nose in too far where he doesn't belong."

Clint took another look around. Once he was sure they still weren't being watched, he asked, "Those men are soldiers?"

Muller's body shook as he coughed up a short snort of a laugh. "Not hardly. I said they worked for Varillo, not that they were soldiers. The colonel may be desperate to fill his uniforms, but even he's got his standards.

"They were just hired to put the scare into anyone who came through here that didn't belong. Since this place doesn't get a whole lot of visitors, they pounce pretty hard on them that do wander this way. I've seen 'em put four slugs into a man's back even as he was trying to run away."

Watching the lieutenant, Clint had to struggle with the notion that this man was still an active officer in the United States Army and not some ragged mountain man with an iron stomach. "You watched that, huh?"

"What would you rather have me do?" Muller asked, his voice dropping to a deadly serious note. "Should I have rousted them every time I saw them look cross-eyed at someone? You think I should have played the hero and drawn their attention to me like I did for you?"

Clint didn't answer. He was too busy spotting familiar faces stepping through the front door to discuss ethics with the grizzled veteran.

"I had to live in this damn hellhole for the last four months just so I wouldn't get any more strange looks when I crossed the street," Muller said in a harsh whisper. "My men are scattered all around this town and have been sleeping in the ground or in rat-infested cellars just so that we could all be in place once this day arrived. This is bigger than a few strangers getting themselves killed by some local trash. This place is a fuse and once it's lit, the whole damn country explodes."

TWENTY-FOUR

Every one of Clint's senses were on the alert. While he listened to what Lieutenant Muller was saying, he watched as more and more of the gunmen from outside stepped into the saloon and took up positions around the room. He could feel the grain on the Colt's grip as his hand slid down toward his holster and the smell of burning wood filled the air.

"Your squad's already here?" Clint asked.

Nodding, Muller said, "That's right. They're waiting in town and hidden in the hills all around it."

"So why haven't you moved in yet? It wouldn't take much to clear out Varillo's men here and then you could move south."

"Just pick them off as we go. Is that it? Then Varillo could pull back and hide for another couple years. We need to get inside his camp and we can't afford to wait any longer."

Clint nodded toward the locals who were coming in closer. "Looks like we're not the only ones tired of waiting."

Without even looking toward the front of the saloon, Muller nodded. "They won't make their move until the

rest of them get in here. Once that happens, they'll sur-
round us and start shooting."

"Great. Sounds about right. Do you have a way worked
out for us to get out of here or should I just step through
one of the windows?"

"Actually, I had two things in mind," Muller said without even the hint of worry on his voice. "First, we get
ourselves to some safer ground, and then you'll see just
why this filthy town is so important to Varillo in the first
place."

Ignoring the semicircle of gunmen closing in on him
from all sides, Muller got up and started walking toward
one of the many gaping holes in the saloon's walls. His
peg leg knocked against the floor like a single dry knuckle,
yet he maneuvered without stumbling once on the uneven
surface.

Clint followed closely behind, being careful not to let
any of the gunmen get too close without nailing them with
a deathly stare. The lieutenant ducked his head to walk
outside through a hole that had rotted through the side of
the building. As soon as he was past the wall, he turned
sharply to the left and headed for the rear of the building.
It was all Clint could do to keep up without losing sight
of the man.

After turning the corner, Clint spotted Muller leaning
against the side of the neighboring building. His back was
pressed against the base of a chimney that was only
slightly wider than his shoulders and made out of filthy,
soot-covered stones. The masonry used to run along the
side of a house that must have been at least two floors
high, possibly more than that with an attic. Although the
chimney still stood with only a few decaying spots near
the top, most of the house it had served to warm had fallen
away to a pile of rubble.

Listening to the sounds of footsteps drawing closer with
every passing second, Clint watched as Lieutenant Muller

held out a single finger, touched it to one of the bricks
behind him just below waist level, and pushed in. The
section of brick moved grudgingly, letting out a puff of
smoky dust as stone grated against decayed mortar.

Before Clint could figure out what was going on, the
section of chimney Muller was leaning against fell back
into the bricks. Muller brought his arms in close to his
body, stepped back with his good leg, and dropped straight
down into the ground.

Clint could see that the chimney section was already
sliding back into place, so he ran forward and stepped into
the dark rectangular hole before it got too small for him
to fit. His stomach jumped up to the back of his throat as
he immediately began falling through empty air.

Almost instantly, the toe of his boot smacked against
something solid. Immediately after that, the entire front
part of his body found that solid object as well. First his
knees pounded against it, which sent hot flashes of pain
up through his legs. After that, his hands came up reflexively just in time to keep his nose from being flattened
against the cool, smooth surface.

The darkness faded away into the dim glow of firelight
as Clint's body continued to slide downward. Ignoring the
pain caused by his knees and bare hands scraping along
metal, he managed to flip himself onto his back just as he
reached the end of what appeared to be an oversized coal
chute.

When he looked up, Clint spotted Muller nearby, looking down on him with open amusement and pulling himself up to a standing position. In the next instant, Clint also
spotted several figures crouching in the shadows. The more
he looked for them, the more he found. And judging by
the way the air howled through the space in every direction, there was enough room to hold a small army.

"Mister Adams," Muller said once he got up. "I'd like
to introduce you to the Ghost Squadron."

TWENTY-FIVE

As Clint watched, the shadows around him were slowly dispelled by lanterns strategically placed on the walls and floor. Although the flickering light didn't spread to all corners of the room, it did a good job of letting him know just how many others were in there with him.

He wasn't about to count them all, but Clint guessed there had to be dozens of them spread out inside the cool space. From what he could tell, they were gathered in some kind of cave or mine shaft. The walls seemed chiseled in places, but rough and natural in others. Overhead, a couple of wooden beams spanned the ceiling and the metal chute that had dropped him below the street stretched all the way past the lanterns' reach.

"Thanks a lot, Adams," Muller said. "I made a bet with my men that I could ride that plate of tin and land better than you . . . half-leg and all." Reaching down to offer Clint a hand in getting up, he winked and lifted Clint to his feet. "You nearly broke your face, but you did manage to win me ten dollars."

At first, the sound was like water rushing through an underground stream. Then, when it built up to a louder pitch, it could be recognized as voices . . . many of them . . .

rustling in the darkness until they rose to the sound of hushed laughter.

Once the laughter broke, men came streaming in toward Muller, embracing him in open arms and slapping him heartily on the back. The lieutenant swapped greetings with several of the others and then turned back to face Clint.

"Don't fret it none," he said. "I damn near killed myself on that thing the first time I tried it."

Now that Clint was fairly certain he wasn't in any immediate danger, he spun around to get a good look at his surroundings. There wasn't a whole lot to see that he hadn't caught the first time, although there did seem to be more men gathered here than he'd originally thought. Even with the figures closing in next to him and Muller, there were still plenty more shifting in the darkness. Before too long, more lanterns started flaring up farther down the tunnel.

"Where the hell are we?" Clint asked once the noise of all the other voices died down a bit.

Muller stepped through the growing crowd of men. Already, the rest of the group seemed to be dispersing through the cave and getting on with their own business. "Come on," Muller said while heading down the passage. "I'll fill you in as we go."

As Clint and Muller walked, the cavern around them closed in until it was just wide enough for them to walk side by side. The ceiling was about nine feet high and was held up in spots by thick pieces of timber. To add to the claustrophobic feel of the place, there was a constant flow of other men bumping Clint's shoulder or nudging him aside as they passed. Not a single one of them put a hand on Muller or even so much as asked him to move.

"This started out as a mine," Muller said after picking up a lantern and heading down the tunnel. "But the digging

crews started getting spooked by sounds they heard while
they worked. They swore this place was haunted and the
dead were howling from where they were buried in the
local cemetery less than a quarter mile away from the entrance.

"Since nobody ever struck much of anything down here,
the owner picked up and moved on. A while later, a government survey crew found that the mine cut into a natural
cavern."

Just then, they passed near a beam of light, which was
spilling in from a crack originating too far over their heads
to see. A stray breeze whistled through the cave and let
out a low, whistling moan that echoed on down the passage.

"There's your restless dead," Muller explained. "We've
been using this place as a base of operations since we
started working our way into the town up above. The government's been keeping these tunnels under their hats because they were so close to the border. Makes 'em perfect
for smuggling."

"Smuggling?" Clint asked. "Which way?"

"Name it. Guns and liquor, to and from Mexico. Picking
up refugees trying to make it into America. Or even just
storing supplies as an emergency reserve. After all . . . you
just never know."

"How far do they go?"

"There's still crews working their way south and north-
east. This tunnel here goes all the way into Mexico. Which
is, by the way, exactly why I'm telling you all of this."

"I was wondering when you'd get to that."

Muller stopped and put his hands on his hips. Even in
the meager light, beads of sweat could be seen trickling
down his face. His ragged breathing sounded like a bel-
lows in the stony confines. "This is one hell of a system.
Only problem is that we're not the only ones that know
about it."

"Varillo?"

Nodding, the lieutenant wiped at his forehead with a dark bandanna. "Yep. We caught the first one of his men down here a couple weeks ago. Lord only knows how long he's been using these tunnels before then."

"This old mine seems pretty crowded. How could you miss any extra visitors?"

"It's like I said before. My men and I only just got here. Before us, there's only the spare scout that checks the place. Other than that, Varillo could've held a party down here every night of the week for all we knew. And if he's got a line on this place, that means he's had a free ride across the border to set up any arrangements he might have wanted."

"Not to mention whatever other ways he has of sneaking around," Clint added.

To that, Muller could only nod. "I'm an army man. The Service sneaks around too much for my tastes. Hell, they talked about this passage like it wasn't no big deal."

"Which means they're worried about something else."

"Well, that something else has got to be big, because the last time we were sent packing so quickly, we damn near went to war."

Clint started to ask for more details, but then stopped himself. Sometimes, he knew, it was better not to know.

TWENTY-SIX

When the sun set on West Texas, it turned the landscape into something almost alien to the rest of the country. Times like those made it a little easier for travelers to understand why native Texans looked upon their state as an entirely different country.

The terrain became harsh and desolate. Every bit of warm detail was washed away by the night, leaving nothing more than a barren land, which was even harsh to look at. Still, it possessed a certain charm that could be appreciated by the right set of eyes. Having been born and raised in Texas, Gerard Lantiss had those eyes. And when he looked out at the moon-drenched landscape, he saw something cool and inviting.

Then again, he also saw the beauty in a finely polished dagger sliding through warm flesh.

Although he could have arrived in Perro Rojo earlier in the day, just before sundown, he'd purposely slowed his pace so that he would arrive after dusk. All the better to make his entrance with a minimum of fuss. Even if he was one of the few people who didn't live in the sorry excuse for a town, who could ride in without so much as a second glance, Lantiss still preferred to come and go without being noticed.

Especially this time.

This wasn't just any trip to the border. This was to be his final trip to the border and quite possibly the final time his boots touched American soil. As much as he would miss Texas, Lantiss knew he wouldn't miss America one bit.

Sensing it was close to its destination, Lantiss's horse picked up its pace until it felt the bit being pulled deeper into its mouth by its rider. Shaking its head from side to side, the animal let out a huffing breath and resumed its previous gait.

Behind the gunman, Rebecca was looking toward the town, swearing she could feel the bile rising up to the back of her throat. She knew better than to express her distaste for being here, but wasn't about to let her misery go unnoticed.

"Jesus, hasn't this place blown away yet?" she asked in a disgusted voice.

Lantiss smiled to himself. "Soon," he muttered over his shoulder. "It will all happen soon enough."

Bringing his horse to a stop about twenty yards away from the closest building, Lantiss swung down from the saddle and led the animal in the rest of the way by its reins. Without the benefit of sunlight, the town made him feel like a tiny insect walking through a graveyard. Each building loomed over him, marking the spot where something had died, teetering noisily in the meandering winds that crossed over the West Texas trails.

When he got to the first building, Lantiss motioned for Rebecca to ride past him. She did so without even glancing at the signals she was being given. Lantiss was lucky that he'd told her to do exactly what she was about to do on her own. Rebecca rode down Perro Rojo's single street and headed for the third squat pile of spare wood on the right.

Within seconds after she'd passed, someone had stepped out from the shadows of an empty door frame. The figure watched her go before knocking on the side of the building and hurrying off in her wake. That figure was joined by another and then another. By the time Rebecca made it to where she'd been headed, there was a group of three men coming straight toward her.

She turned around and looked at them without so much as a flicker of surprise showing on her face. The only reaction she had was to roll her eyes, pull a bag off her horse's back, and start walking toward the building.

The man in front of the other two seemed particularly amused by this and jogged up until he was directly behind her. "Hey there, lady," he whispered. "Kinda late to be out on yer own, ain't it?"

There was the click of a hammer being pulled back, which caused the man's eyes to suddenly become wide as saucers.

"She's not alone," came Lantiss's voice from the shadows behind the other three.

For a second, the trio froze. They were unwilling to even move their eyes away from Rebecca, who seemed more than a little amused by their predicament. Turning on her heel, she carried her bag into the building and shut the door behind her.

"Turn around," Lantiss hissed.

When the men complied, he holstered his gun, looked at the middle man straight in the eyes . . . and slapped him so hard that the sound of it echoed down the street. Although there was an angry fire burning in the local man's eyes, he didn't even start to try and fight back.

Lantiss stepped up to the man and glared at him until he saw the local back away. With his dominance asserted, he said, "You boys are getting sloppy. Now tell me what you saw around here or I'll hire me a new set of guards for this place."

TWENTY-SEVEN

Clint and Muller had only been walking for a few minutes, but the farther they went, the more the cavern seemed to close in around them. Although he wasn't much of a miner, Clint had seen his share of the insides of underground tunnels and had even been forced to spend a few nights in a cave. But that didn't mean he enjoyed any of it.

By the way Muller was slowing down and starting to wheeze when he exhaled, he was starting to feel the same way. "Damn," he said after coming to a stop near a spot where the passage went into a sharp curve. "Every time I come down here, these tunnels seem to get smaller and smaller."

"I was just thinking that myself," Clint said. "It will be nice to have the entire sky over my head again." The more he thought about it, the more Clint's lungs ached for a breath of fresh air. Inside the renovated mine shaft, every breath left a damp, musty taste in the back of his throat. Each step wore away at the soles of his feet since there was nothing between himself and solid rock but the leather of his boots.

His eyes had become somewhat accustomed to the near

darkness, but Clint was starting to feel the strain of having to constantly struggle to see in the meager illumination given off by the lantern. "Where are we headed?" he asked. "Or is that classified information, too?"

Muller's laugh echoed down the passage in both directions before the sound came back at them as though it was sneaking up on both of the men. "The rest of my squadron is camped out near one of the smaller outlets. We need to join up with them and then we can head over the border the old-fashioned way. I'm getting too old to live as a damn mole for more than an hour or two at a stretch."

"So there's more of your squadron than the ones I saw down here?"

"Definitely."

"How many all together?"

"Now that, I'm afraid, is something I can't tell you."

Clint shook his head slowly. Whenever he dealt with anything connected to Jim or Jeremy West, he knew there would be some things he would never know. There were plenty of things that West didn't even know. But that was still an uneasy transition to make when a man like Clint was so used to running everything in his life according to his rules. Like every other good poker player, Clint prided himself on having a pretty good idea about what all the other players were holding. Now, as exciting as this new game was, the rules were starting to get under his skin.

"How do you keep it all straight?" Clint asked.

"Keep what straight?"

"The secrets. How do you remember what you can tell people and what you can't? After a while, don't you just tend to start talking too much or not at all?"

This time, rather than laugh, Muller let out a deep sigh. He sounded tired physically as well as mentally and the simple act of exhaling that one time seemed to take a lot out of him. "After so many years in this kind of life, your gut seems to know a helluva lot more than your head sometimes. I couldn't give you a list of all the things I know or have seen, but the stories are all still there. And so is the knowledge.

"Actually, I was just about to ask you the same thing about your life. I mean, if even half the things I've heard about you are true, than you must've seen some wild things."

"That's true enough."

"How do you keep it all from getting to you?" Muller asked, his voice heavy with genuine curiosity. "I mean a soldier like me kills in the line of duty. I've killed plenty and can still see their faces. But you . . . I mean . . . a gunfighter has to get a little closer than a man like me. Shooting someone down face-to-face isn't the same as on a battlefield. War is a bloody mess, but a straight gunfight is more . . . personal."

"You know something? I don't think I've ever quite thought of it like that," Clint said. He took a moment to mull over the lieutenant's words and found that there was a whole lot of truth packed into them. Because he never jumped feetfirst into a fight, Clint was forced to look a little deeper into the eyes of the men he went up against. While that might have served his morals just fine, it was also a curse.

His kills were made face-to-face. Most of the time, he was there to watch as the last breath leaked out of the dying bodies. To this day, he could still dredge up the faces of every man he'd shot. Maybe not all at once, but they were still there inside of him, yelling at him sometimes during a hard night's sleep.

If any one of them had lived, Clint knew that he most likely would be the one buried six feet under. But that didn't make their memory any easier to bear.

"We're both soldiers in a way," Muller said, the sound of his voice breaking Clint out of his thoughts. "We just fight different wars for different people."

"I'm not at war."

Muller stopped and studied Clint for a second. He moved his eyes over Clint's features as if he was soaking in every aspect. When he looked back at Clint's face, there was a new air about him, almost as though the lieutenant had come to some sort of understanding.

"West told me a lot about you," Muller said. "He said you'll fight the good fight and that you'll back the right play. With the type of people trying to grab for power in this world, that's an awful lot to take on sometimes. It may not be war in the literal sense, but it's damn close."

Clint felt a reflexive response to disagree with Muller. But the old soldier was simply hitting too close to the mark for him to argue. So, rather than argue or pursue the subject any further, Clint did the next best thing. "How much farther until we reach camp?"

Muller chuckled a bit under his breath and started walking again at a brisk pace. "Now you see why men like us prefer action to words. Most of the time, I'd rather take the bullet than talk about pulling the trigger."

TWENTY-EIGHT

The rest of the underground walk was made in relative silence. Clint and Muller made casual conversation, but nothing that lasted more than a few sentences swapped in quick bits and pieces. Since the tunnels were getting progressively more narrow every hundred feet or so, they were soon too busy trying to keep the top of their heads from bouncing off the rock to worry about idle chitchat.

Finally, Muller turned down a passage that was so cramped they were forced to stoop over and shuffle like two geese in a row before reaching a dead end. Once there, Muller held the lantern close to the wall and began running his hand carefully along the rough surface.

"I know it's around here somewhere," he muttered more to himself than Clint. "These damn tunnels all start to look alike after a while, it's nearly enough to drive me cr—"

Suddenly, Muller found the right spot on the rockface and a jagged piece of it gave way beneath his fingertips. There was a muffled *click* before the back of Clint's neck was lightly dusted with powder and bits of gravel rained down on him from above.

If he had enough room to move, Clint would have looked up to see where the falling debris had come from.

Instead, all he could do was watch as Muller straightened up in front of him and started scaling the wall. At first, it looked as though the lieutenant was being pulled up into the ceiling, but then Clint was able to make out small indentations that had been made in the rock wall. They weren't much more than deep dents that had been filled up with dirt and covered by what appeared to be spider webs. But once Muller used them to work his way up the wall and out of the shaft, it was obvious the dents were arranged in a pattern to be used as hand- and footholds. In fact, with his peg leg fitting easily into the holds, this was the only part of the trip that was easier for Muller to make.

The moment he could shuffle forward, Clint stepped up to the wall and was immediately rewarded with a gust of fresh air coming from over his head. Although his back, knees, and neck protested painfully, he straightened up and took a look at the top of the shaft.

Muller was just crawling out of the way as Clint craned his neck upward. The shaft went straight up and ended in a small square opening. His eyes adjusted to the darkness, Clint could see the stars burning in the sky. The cool touch of the air on his cheeks was more than enough to energize him for the climb ahead.

Reaching up for the highest dent in the wall he could find, Clint managed to get his fingers in just past the first joint and pull himself up a foot or so. As soon as his boot found one of the lower dents, he lifted up a bit more and was inside the vertical shaft.

Almost immediately, he realized that the space was even tighter than he'd thought. But since the dents in the wall were barely deep enough to use, the fact that he could press his back against the side of the passage gave him just enough leverage to work his way toward the top.

Like the walk from where he'd entered the caverns, the climb up out of them seemed much longer than it actually

was. After only a couple minutes of climbing, Clint felt as
though he'd been clawing his way up that wall for hours.
By the time his face came out of the hole and into the
open air, every muscle in his arms and legs were crying
for mercy.

At that moment, Clint felt a pair of hands grab hold of
him beneath the arms from behind to pull him the rest of
the way up. After being lifted from the hole like a cork
from a bottle, Clint almost dropped to his knees out of
sheer exhaustion.

"That's a helluva way to travel, ain't it?"

The voice sounded like it was being spoken from behind
a waterfall. It took a moment for Clint to realize that the
rushing sound he heard over everything else was the blood
running through his head. After catching his breath, the
sound faded away and he turned to face the man who'd
spoken.

Muller looked back at him wearing a good-natured
smile. "Don't feel too bad," he said. "I've made the trip
several times and I still ain't used to it."

"Sure," said someone from behind Muller. "But you're
also old enough to be any of our granddaddies."

Once Clint's eyes were adjusted to the new open surroundings, he saw that he was standing in what looked like
open trail. The stars were bright overhead and the sky
seemed to go on forever. On either side of him, the land
also seemed to stretch out farther than his eyes could see.
Directly in front of him, however, was a scene much more
cluttered than that.

Lieutenant Muller stood before him, looking him up and
down the way a father might inspect a fallen child. Behind
the older man, a small campfire crackled and snapped, giving off a radiant glow, which dazzled Clint's eyes when
he first caught sight of it. The flames weren't that bright,
but they were just such a stark contrast to the pitch black-

ness of the caverns that it took a few seconds for him to adjust.

Sitting around the fire were easily a dozen men, some of which were gathered around Muller and moving toward Clint. One of these men, a wiry youth in his early twenties wearing a black vest and a black bandanna tied around his neck, was dusting off Muller's shoulders. He'd been the one to make the crack about the lieutenant's age.

Muller wheeled around and smacked the younger man alongside his head with the palm of his hand. "I may be old, Simmons, but I can still kick your sorry ass into next week."

Hearing that, many of the other men started laughing quietly to themselves. Clint got an immediate sense that none of these men were new to the group. Every one of them interacted and talked to each other as though they knew exactly where they stood. Oddly enough, the camp felt more like one belonging to a tightly-knit outlaw gang rather than a military unit.

"How'd that job in Labyrinth go, Simmons?" Muller asked.

"No problem, sir," Simmons said before stepping up to Clint. "So you must be Clint Adams. Heard a lot about you when I was in Labyrinth."

Nodding, Clint said, "Really? Do you mind if I ask what you did in Labyrinth?"

"Sorry. Can't talk about it."

"I figured as much."

"But you'll be glad to know I only heard good things when I was there. I'm sure you'll be worth all the trouble we went through to get you on our side."

"That's what we're here to find out," Muller said from his spot close to the fire. "Now everyone gather round. We got a lot of planning to do."

TWENTY-NINE

Rebecca watched the way Lantiss strutted around the dirty thieves who worked for him. Of Perro Rojo's population, most of them worked directly for Colonel Varillo, while the others made their living serving him in more indirect ways. Whether they were killing for him or carrying his stolen goods over the border, they were all putting money into Varillo's pockets. The way Lantiss walked around the crumbling buildings, one might think that he was behind it all.

But Rebecca knew better. She knew that although Lantiss was a much better killer than the others, he was still a lapdog. While she didn't think too much more about her own position in the colonel's organization, at least she knew where she stood and didn't have any delusions about her spot in the pecking order.

Keeping herself in the shadows, she waited for Lantiss to make his presence known and assert himself on the dogs at his command. After an hour or two slipped away, she realized she'd been forgotten by the other man completely. That was fine, since she had plenty to do on her own that Lantiss had no part of.

After quietly leading her horse away from where Lantiss

was browbeating the hired help, Rebecca made sure she was well out of earshot before climbing into the saddle and touching her heels to the animal's sides. The mare took off at a run, grateful for the chance to stretch her muscles after riding for so long at a plodding walk.

Rebecca took an indirect route toward a group of low hills less than a mile outside of town. Although she knew several ways to check if she was being followed, all of them took too much time. Besides, she would rather not have anyone know that she was anything else besides a dumb showgirl kept around as one of Colonel Varillo's favorite playthings.

Keeping her destination in mind, she rode a couple hundred feet in one direction and then changed her heading as though she was merely wandering through the darkness on a simple joyride. Finally, she found herself close enough to the hills to steer the horse straight for her real destination and snap the reins accordingly.

The animal's hooves beat against the ground in a pounding rhythm, kicking up a cloud of dust that looked more like an inky mist in the black night. She didn't mind that the animal was making more noise than a freight train at this point. In fact, she was counting on the racket to draw the attention of the people she'd come to see.

The moment she rode over the crest of one of the steeper hills, she heard a sharp voice from one of the nearby shadows.

"Stop right there," it said.

Rebecca did as she was told, pulling back on the reins until her horse drew to a halt.

Then, appearing from almost every direction like a bunch of phantoms closing in on her, four shadowy figures emerged from the darkness. They took up positions around her, making sure to keep well enough out of sight so that she couldn't see exactly which ones were armed, or what exactly they were doing.

"Throw down your guns and climb on down from there," one of the figures ordered.

Rebecca slowly lowered herself to the ground and stood with her hands in the air. "I don't have a gun," she said, her voice sugarcoated and trembling slightly.

One of the figures stepped out from hiding. He was about the same height as her, but with a much more angular build. His broad shoulders tapered down to a slim waist, giving him the outline of an upside-down triangle. Dressed in all black, he was directly in front of her before his eyes could be seen at all.

The figure's arm came up with a quick snap of air, pressing a slender blade to her throat. "Don't bullshit me, Rebecca," he said. "We all know damn well that you don't go anywhere without your guns."

"I keep them between my legs," she said. "You want to get them yourself, or should I?"

"You go on ahead," the man replied. The strength in his voice hadn't faltered, but there was a little more strain in there than the first time he'd spoken.

Nodding and lowering her head with false modesty, she undid her jeans and slid them down to the ground, tracing her fingers along the inside of her thighs. When she reached up a little higher, she pulled in a quick breath just loud enough for the men to hear and then pulled her hand back out.

She held a small steel derringer between her fingers, allowing the little two-shot gun to dangle like a dead rat. "Is this what you want?" she asked, knowing damn well what they all wanted.

"Yeah. Toss it over."

Rebecca did as she was told, throwing the pistol toward the first man's feet with a flick of her wrist. Before the gun hit the ground, she'd already drawn the second gun from her other garter. This one was somewhat bigger, but still thin enough to keep hidden. It was a .22, custom-made for her, and could hold four shots in the small cylinder.

The .22 appeared in her hand in the blink of an eye, without so much as a sound to announce its presence. Rebecca could just as easily have removed it the same way she'd done with the derringer, but then she wouldn't have learned so much.

Already, she knew for a fact that she could get the drop on these men with a minimum of effort. She also knew that, if push came to shove, she could outdraw them if necessary.

Wearing a satisfied smile on her face, she straightened her back. She knew that the shirt she was wearing was almost long enough to hide her silk panties from sight. The men in front of her got a quick glimpse of the black panties before Rebecca reached down and pulled her trousers back up.

"Here you go," she said while handing over the .22.

The same man snatched it out of her hand. His eyes lingered on her for an extra moment, however, before he stepped back in line with his partner. Looking toward one of the men behind Rebecca, he asked, "Anyone else coming this way?"

"No," said one of the others. "It's clear."

Finally, the dark man seemed to relax. Tucking Rebecca's .22 into one of his pockets, he said, "All right then. Let's go."

Rebecca followed the four men, who were all dressed in similar black clothing with their skin blotted out as well. Despite the fact that they surrounded her and escorted her down the other side of the hill, she couldn't help but feel like she was the one leading them.

THIRTY

Even with over a dozen men huddled around it, the small campfire was warm enough to make Clint almost forget about trudging a mile through a dank cave. Also, the soldiers had already cooked dinner so he got a healthy portion of beans, bacon, and coffee to top off the night properly.

While he and Muller ate, Clint didn't hear any mention of the Ghost Squadron's mission or his part in it. All the men knew this was one of the few times they could relax and weren't about to let a moment of it go by unappreciated.

Clint was sipping his second cup of coffee when Muller plopped down beside him and tossed his empty plate onto the ground near his feet. "All right, Adams," he grunted. "You should know that you're here for something else besides eating my food."

"I was afraid of that."

"I hope West told you about what we need you to do."

Clint nodded. "He said he wanted me to join up with Varillo's men because he was looking for gunfighters and that he would probably be anxious to have someone who'd already made a name for themselves working for him."

"So far so good. That was the plan originally, but Var-

123

illo's been stepping things up recently. Even since we got
here, the troops across the border have been inching north
bit by bit, day by day. It's not quite the start of an invasion,
but he sure is working up to it." Muller fished the stump
of a cigar from his shirt pocket. One end was charred while
the other was chewed. "I think of our colonel as a dog,
crawling up as close as he can get to the rabbits so he
doesn't have to jump so far to sink his teeth in."

"Does Varillo know he's being watched?" Clint asked.

Leaning forward with the cigar clenched between his
teeth, Muller nearly stuck his face into the fire and held it
there for a second. When he pulled it back, the tip of his
cigar glowed brightly and sent wisps of foul smoke drifting
up into his face.

The lieutenant shrugged after taking a few puffs. "He
might know or he might not. At this point, it really doesn't
matter. That's why I've been sending out patrols whose
only job is to be spotted by the enemy."

Before Clint could ask, Muller reached down and drew
a line in the dirt ringing the fire. "Varillo's forces are all
along the border here and here," he said while stabbing at
points along the crude map he'd drawn. "The patrols I've
been sending out have only been to this area here, leaving
the rest to be watched by the rest of my men. If Varillo
knows about them, then I might as well retire. Those
scouts are the best in the country.

"Since he knows we're watching one area, Varillo's
been sending his men in the opposite direction. Once we
get enough of them there, that's when we can sweep down,
take them by surprise, and wipe out enough of his army
that it'll take him two lifetimes to rebuild."

"So where do I come in?"

"You ride in through here," Muller explained while tracing a line between the two major hot spots he'd already
marked. "Once you cross into Mexico, finding Varillo's
army ain't too hard."

"Yeah," said one of the troops sitting around the fire. "Just look for the blue jackets and the big guns. They'll be the ones trying to kill you on sight."

Ignoring the comment, Muller went on to say, "Convince whoever you have to that you want to join and see if you can work your way toward the encampments near the border where Varillo thinks he's safe."

"You mean the ones he thinks aren't being watched?"

"You got it. Once you're there, learn all you can from the inside and get out. But don't forget that once you try to leave, Varillo will know something's wrong. That's when you shift into the last phase of your mission and become our barbed arrow."

"Barbed arrow?"

Muller nodded. "We make our attack in four days. That gives you a day or two to get in and another day or so to see what you can see. By the time you're heading out, the fight will be on, which should make it even easier for you to get the hell out of there in the middle of all the commotion. We'll need your intelligence report to decide how best to wrap up Varillo's men, but more importantly, we need you to hit him hard on your way out.

"Just like a barbed arrow. He'll know you're there and he'll want you out of his army. You just make sure to tear up as much of it as you can before you're out. If you tear him up enough, we'll be able to finish him off that much quicker."

Muller sat back and worked on his cigar, giving his words a few seconds to sink in.

Clint's mind raced with so many different things, even though he knew that he would have to make up most of what he was to do as he went along. Although he was no stranger to working so close to the vest, it didn't do much to help him feel better about the mission as a whole.

"Of course, before we do any of that, we need to introduce you to one of Varillo's officers and through him, we'll get close enough to do the rest." Muller leaned back and looked at Clint expectantly. "So what do you think, Adams?"

Taking a moment to look around, Clint could see that the eyes of every other soldier around the fire were trained on him. Finally, before the tension rose another notch, he took one more sip of his coffee and tossed the rest into the fire.

"I think I made a big mistake letting Jeremy talk me into this," Clint said plainly. "Odds are good that I'll get killed before I can do much of anything and they're even better that I'll get killed on my way out."

For the next few moments, the men around the campfire were completely silent. Then, after exchanging a few glances among one another, they all burst out into laughter. Of all the men in the camp, Muller was laughing the loudest.

"I gotta hand it to ya, Adams," the lieutenant said once he caught his breath. "You sure tell it like it is. In fact, that's exactly what the other barbed arrows said before you joined up with us."

"How many others were there?" Clint asked.

And just as suddenly as it had appeared, the humor on Muller's face was gone. "Five. All of them were my men and not a one of them will be coming home."

"That's good to hear. So what makes you think that I'll have any better luck than the others?"

"Because they didn't have your reputation. And they didn't have your skills at working alone. My men are damn good soldiers, but Varillo's never heard of any one of them by themselves. You, on the other hand, are the Gunsmith. He'll snatch you up like you were gift-wrapped and waiting for him under his Christmas tree."

Clint stared down at the dying embers of the fire, poking at some of the burning logs with a twig. The other soldiers seemed to have found other things to do by this point, leaving his and Muller's conversation as private as it could be with all things considered.

Turning his head toward the lieutenant, Clint broke the short silence. "You're the one who asked for me, aren't you?"

"How's that?"

"When Jeremy West came to me, he said he was too busy for this assignment and asked if I could take it over for him. That's not the reason I'm here, is it? You got me down here personally to do this."

"And so what if I did? Does that change anything?"

"No. But it does give me a little better idea of who I'm dealing with. In fact, that you could rope me into this so quickly actually makes me feel a little better about working for you." Clint held out his hand, which was immediately accepted by Muller. "You're a resourceful man, Lieutenant. Now how do you plan on getting me into Varillo's good graces in such a short time?"

Muller's grin brought the cigar nub up close to the side of his nose. "Oh, that's easy. You're gonna impress him by doing something that will not only impress the hell out of him, but show him where your loyalties are."

"Which is?"

"Killing me, of course."

THIRTY-ONE

Once Rebecca was led down the slope of the last hill, she could see a campfire no more than fifty feet away. Sitting around it were several men who appeared to be finishing up dinner, while all around in the darkness were patrols of various sizes dressed to blend in with the shadows in a similar manner as her escorts.

"Wait here," the man directly in front of Rebecca ordered. He then jogged on up to the campfire, leaving the other three men in black to make sure she didn't budge from her spot.

Rebecca stayed put as commanded and took the next couple of minutes to study the meager encampment. As hard as she tried, she was unable to pick out just how many men were in the area. Whenever she thought she had a fairly accurate count, she would spot another small group lurking in the darkness or another couple solitary figures, which might have been cactus just as easily as they could have been snipers.

Just as Rebecca had stopped trying to scout any further, her head escort came running back to her side.

"Come on," he said. "He'll see you now."

Rebecca made sure to at least put on the façade of respectfulness and hold her tongue before making any smart comments about a campfire in the middle of nowhere being treated like some kind of royal court. So she followed without saying a word until she was close enough to the fire to start feeling some of its heat.

Once she was there, she walked right up to a pair of figures seated with their backs to her. Although one of them seemed vaguely familiar, she knew which one she'd come to see. Reaching down, she tapped the bulkier of the two on the shoulder.

"Here I am, Paul," she said. "Sorry I'm a little late."

"Not at all," the man said. "I was just talking things over with a new friend of mine." Struggling to stand up, the figure turned around and wrapped his arms around Rebecca. "Let me introduce you two. Rebecca Chase, this is—"

"Clint Adams," she said, finishing the man's sentence as soon as she got a good look at the other person's face.

Clint was up on his feet in no time, looking between Rebecca and Muller before offering his hand. "Yes . . . we've met. I see you got yourself out of Rick's Place before things got too hectic."

"Not before watching you for a little while. I must say, you put on quite a show."

Thinking back to the low-cut dress Rebecca had been wearing the last time he'd seen her, Clint said, "So do you. How much did you manage to fleece those card players for?"

Rebecca grinned and lowered her head as though she'd just been paid a compliment. "No more than they could afford to lose. Besides, the money didn't go into my pockets. Not all of it, anyway."

"Anything for charity, huh?"

"Something like that."

Rebecca and Clint looked into each other's eyes, each one studying the other like two foxes comparing notes.

Finally, they were interrupted by a rough hand on each of their shoulders.

"Well, I see that you two have a lot to catch up on," Muller said. "So I'll just leave you to it. Clint, we head out before sunup tomorrow morning, so try to get as much sleep as you can. And Rebecca . . . try to let Clint get as much sleep as he can."

The lieutenant turned and headed away from the fire. There were several other men already sleeping in their bedrolls on a patch of ground near the middle of the camp. Muller walked that way, becoming just another shadow stirring in the darkness once he wandered too far away from the fire.

Rebecca cast her eyes downward, examining Clint's body before looking back up into his eyes. "I guess I have my orders. It was nice meeting you again, Mister Adams."

Clint nodded. "It sure was."

"Something tells me we'll be seeing more of each other before too long."

"That's funny. I was just thinking the same thing."

Clint watched her leave, enjoying the way Rebecca's body moved within the awkward confines of her riding clothes. Even though she was dressed in dirty pants and a shirt that was several sizes too big, she still held herself as though she was still in one of her finest gowns. Her hips swayed back and forth, every step she took letting Clint know that she was certain he was watching her.

Unable to take his eyes off of her until she was enveloped in shadows, Clint walked over to one of the nearby sentries who told him where he could find an extra bedroll for the night. The accommodations were far from perfect, but being under the stars again in the crisp night air was more than enough to make up for resting his back against the cold ground.

Even as Clint's eyelids became heavier and the weight of the last couple of days pushed him closer into sleep, he knew he wouldn't be able to rest very soundly. There was simply too much for his mind to digest before he could allow himself any degree of comfort. There was too much going on that he couldn't control. Too many factors that were out of his reach.

The more he thought about it, the more it seemed to overwhelm him. And the more he tried not to think about it, the more he couldn't help circling back to it.

Finally, after his head started to spin beneath it all, Clint drifted off into unconsciousness.

And during the hours when his eyes were closed, his hand remained on the grip of his Colt. More than once, he nearly drew the pistol in response to a heavy footstep or even the call of an animal. Already, he'd put himself in the frame of mind required to survive the task before him. And still, something deep down inside told him it might not be enough.

THIRTY-TWO

Walking away from the campfire, Rebecca could feel Clint's eyes roaming over her body. She shifted her hips in just the right way, imagining what it would feel like once his hands were on them. Closing her eyes for a moment, she let her own hand drift to her leg, gently tracing her fingertips up until they grazed her upper thigh. Then, before she got too far, she opened her eyes and let both arms swing freely at her sides.

She was in the dark now, moving through shadows that were of the thick, soupy variety only found miles away from civilization. The shadows wrapping around this place were the kind that made a person realize why he'd been afraid of the dark as a child. But Rebecca used that little flutter of fear in the pit of her stomach to drive her forward, hastening her steps until she was at the side of one of the soldiers sitting alone at the edge of camp.

"I heard they brought you in, Rebecca," the soldier said. "Stabbed anyone in the back lately?"

Rebecca eased up to the soldier and slipped her hands around his waist. "Oh, Mason. Why would you talk that way to me?"

Even with his face covered in the black mixture of paint

and mud, Mason's expression was clear enough. His thin lips were drawn into a tight frown. Narrow, blue eyes shone through the camouflage to pierce Rebecca all the way through to the core. "I just call them like I see 'em. There ain't no reason to trust spies."

Running her hands along his midsection, Rebecca dug at his waistband until she could slip her fingers up beneath his shirt. Once there, she pressed her palms against his tensed stomach and gently raked her fingernails over his skin. "You're saying one thing, but I get the feeling that you mean something else." She slipped her thumbs down the front of his pants and unfastened the clasp. "You really don't think I'm all that bad, do you?"

Mason drew in a deep breath, his eyes narrowing just a little more. "Who knows what you tell Varillo or his men when you're over there? Just because you come back here and rat them out doesn't make you any easier to trust."

Pulling open his pants, Rebecca slipped her hand down along his stomach until she could feel the base of his penis. She kept her fingers in that spot, lingering just so he could feel how close she was to touching him there. "What can I do to make you feel better about me?" she whispered. "What can I do to make you trust me?"

As much as he wanted to resist, Mason couldn't keep his hands off of her. After setting down his rifle, he placed his hands on her hips and then started tugging her shirt open to reveal a tighter cotton shirt beneath. The fabric clung to her breasts, holding them tightly against her body as his hands roamed over them. Her nipples grew hard the moment he touched them, causing Rebecca to pull in a quick gasp of air.

"It don't matter if I trust you," he said. "It never did. You still find me whenever you check in with the lieutenant and we still wind up like this."

Rebecca never took her hands off his body. Now that his cock had grown hard, she was cupping him in both hands, massaging him in slow, hard strokes. "I kind of like it that you don't trust me. It makes me feel like I might be in danger. Like you might do something to me at any moment."

Suddenly, Mason grabbed hold of her with both hands and tossed her onto the ground. In the next instant, he was kneeling over her, straddling her waist. "So can I trust you?" he asked while tearing off the rest of his clothes.

Rebecca reached down and slid her pants down past her hips, lifting her buttocks just high enough so that the warm patch of hair between her legs pressed up against Mason's shaft. "Does any of that matter?"

"Not at all."

"Then stop asking so many questions and fuck me."

Mason didn't even look at the rest of the campsite, which was no more than fifty feet away. For a moment, he thought that one of the other sentries might hear what he and Rebecca were doing, but that only made him want to do it that much more.

She writhed beneath him, letting her hands explore his body, feeling the difference in texture on his skin where the black paste stopped and his bare flesh began. Wriggling one leg free from beneath his weight, she raised it in the air and then set it down upon his shoulder.

Without missing a beat, Mason grabbed hold of her calf and massaged the sinewy muscles between his fingers. As his hand worked its way down toward her thigh, he could feel his cock getting harder. And by the time his fingers found her hot, moist pussy, all he had to do was fit himself inside and thrust his hips forward, causing them both to grunt with satisfaction.

Keeping his hand in place, Mason rubbed his thumb over her clit as he pumped deep inside her. Rebecca's other leg wrapped around his waist, pulling herself closer while urging him to push deeper between her thighs. Once she'd lifted her hips off the ground, Mason grabbed hold of her tight buttocks with both hands, pulling her toward him while thrusting forward.

Rebecca propped herself up on her elbows, gazing hungrily at Mason while he pounded between her legs. Her pussy was so wet, she could feel the juices dripping down her thighs, allowing him to slide into her even deeper . . . even harder.

With every muscle in his body straining to bring another moan to Rebecca's lips, Mason felt as though he was about to cry out himself. When he set her hips down for a moment, she pulled away from him and got up on her knees.

She didn't say word. Instead, she crawled on the ground and turned so that she was facing in the opposite direction, pressing her chest to the earth while lifting her buttocks high in the air. Savoring the feel she got by offering herself so bluntly to her lover, Rebecca clawed at the ground like a cat, her entire body aching to feel him slide into her once again.

Mason watched her for as long as he could. The line of her body was a smooth, rounded curve, going down along her rump and tapering into the fine slope of her spine. Even in the near-total darkness, he could see the glistening wetness between her legs. He could smell the musky odor of her, which was enough to break his resolve and draw him to her.

Grabbing hold of her hips, Mason pushed his cock between her legs until it slid into her creamy depths. The first time he plunged into her, he did so in one, slow motion that didn't stop until his hips bumped against her soft behind. Then, as the primal part of him took over, Mason thrust into her with more vigor, pulling her hips toward him so that their flesh pounded against each other as waves of pleasure shook both of them all the way down to the bone.

When Rebecca snapped her head up, she made fists in the dirt as though she thought she had to hang on while

Mason rode her. She was nearly unable to keep her voice down when Mason reached forward and grabbed her hair, pulling it back just enough so she could feel it, his cock slamming again and again between her thighs.

The closer she came to orgasm, the harder Rebecca fought to keep the scream from coming out of her mouth. It wasn't due to any amount of shame or embarrassment for what she was doing and where, but merely a test of her own resolve that intensified the sensations coursing throughout her body. And when she finally did climax, she bit down on her lower lip and clenched her fists as wave after wave of pleasure tore beneath her flesh.

Mason kept himself from crying out, but just barely. Pounding into her one last time, he exploded inside of her, clenching her waist in his hands until the feeling worked its way out of his system.

Before dropping onto the ground in exhaustion, he tugged on his pants and threw on his shirt without worrying about any of the buttons. He lay on his back and watched as millions of stars seemed to spin over his head.

A minute later, he could feel Rebecca lying down beside him, resting her head upon his chest.

"It gets better every time I see you," she said quietly.

As much as he hated to admit it, Mason nodded and let his hand drift over her silken hair. "It does at that. But I still say I can't trust you."

Rebecca playfully smacked him on the chin and snuggled in a little closer. "Your precious lieutenant isn't anywhere he can hear you right now. You don't have to keep up with that kind of talk. Besides, it makes me feel bad to hear you say those things."

Mason didn't say anything right away. Before waiting too long, however, he spoke in a softer tone. "You know what I mean. I still don't like you working so close to the likes of Varillo."

"Me, neither, but it's my job." After taking a few moments to trace slow circles on his skin, she asked, "How long will you be posted here?"

"Not long. Actually, I'll be riding out before dawn."

"Really?" She nuzzled in closer until her lips were almost touching Mason's ear. "In that case, there's a favor I need to ask. Actually, I just need to borrow a few things."

THIRTY-THREE

Clint wasn't sure if he even allowed himself to fall asleep during the night. He heard some strange noises at different times, but nothing that was loud enough to get him on his feet. Several times, he wanted to get up and stretch his legs, but then he would roll over and try to drift off all over again.

By the time other soldiers besides the sentries started moving about, Clint decided it was getting close to dawn. While he was working out the numerous kinks in his back and neck, he couldn't decide if he'd spent the entire night before looking up at the stars or if he'd simply dreamed about it. Either way, he felt as though his entire body had been put through a meat grinder and it was too late to do anything about it now.

At that moment, Lieutenant Muller strode up to Clint's side and slapped him on the shoulder. "Mornin', Adams. Nothin' like sleeping under God's creation to get a man ready for another day."

"Yeah," Clint grunted as he rubbed a bunch of knotted muscles in the small of his back. "Somehow, I would've preferred sleeping on the bed that someone else created. It would've been a whole lot easier on my bones." Appar-

138

ently, he'd been spending too much time sleeping in soft beds.

"Well, grab some breakfast and get saddled up, because one of my scouts just came back from a town ten miles south of here saying that one of Varillo's field commanders is staying at a hotel there. We need to get you in good with him before he rides out of there later tonight. If this is the man I think it is, he'll be headed to speak with Varillo himself, which is right where you need to be."

"I'm ready to go. My appetite is gone." Clint looked over to the small area outside of camp where the horses were kept. "I hope you've got a decent ride for me to borrow."

"Borrow? You ain't borrowin' nothing."

Clint shot a puzzled look at Muller. Then he noticed that the lieutenant was motioning for him to turn around. When he did, Clint saw a very familiar Darley Arabian stallion being led in his direction.

"Eclipse?"

"That's right," Muller said. "I had a few men go into Perro Rojo and fetch him. They tell me that horse put up quite a fight."

Jogging over to the stallion, Clint patted Eclipse's muzzle and scratched him behind the ears. "I'll bet he did." Just seeing the familiar animal made Clint feel a little better about the mission. In less than half an hour's time, Clint rode south alone, with Muller and a small group of his men to head out behind him an hour later.

The ride down toward the border was quiet and uneventful. In fact, Clint didn't even see a trace of a single person the entire day. Knowing that he was on a fairly common road into Mexico made the lack of activity seem less of a blessing and more of an oddity.

Toward the end of the day, he started looking for any sign of other riders and came up without a single thing to show for his efforts. For the rest of the ride into town, he thought about everything that was supposed to be going on in the area and compared that to the things he was actually seeing.

Something didn't add up.

Although he couldn't say for sure whether he was on to anything he needed to be concerned about, he stored away his suspicions in the back of his mind. Besides, he was almost at the town that Lieutenant Muller had told him about and there were still some things that needed to be done.

The town was one of the last ones on this trail before the border. It was called Paso Santiago and was known as a stopover for outlaws and banditos on their way toward sanctuary in the south. Although Paso Santiago's reputation was widely known, it was still too rough for any kind of law to take hold and anyone foolish enough to accept the post as sheriff there usually lasted about a day and a half before winding up at the end of a rope outside of his own office.

Clint felt more than a little uneasy going there himself, since a place like that would be filled with the type of men who would jump at the chance to take a shot at him. But it also made sense that someone like Varillo would use that as a safe haven in the States and if Muller's plan worked out, Clint wouldn't be in Paso Santiago for very long anyway.

Stopping when he was half a mile outside of town, Clint checked his watch and saw that he'd arrived well ahead of schedule. Muller wasn't due to arrive for another hour, so Clint picked a secluded spot and climbed down from the saddle.

In order for him to "kill" Lieutenant Muller, he needed to be able to shoot the man without actually harming him so the soldiers accompanying him could carry him off.

Accomplishing that wouldn't be too hard . . . not with a little planning ahead, anyway.

Clint plucked three bullets from his gun belt and then went to work on them with a pocketknife. Using the blade, he took out the lead from those shell casings and filled the empty space with a little more packing to make sure the gunpowder didn't spill out. He went through the process with one shell, loaded it into his Colt and fired it toward the ground.

The pistol went off a little louder than normal, but only made a small dent in the earth as that extra bit of packing bounced against the soil. As long as Clint didn't fire the blank shells directly into Muller's face, the lieutenant should survive their staged shoot-out quite nicely.

Clint went ahead and prepared a few more of the shells and loaded them into his Colt, making sure there were a few live rounds in the cylinder just in case he needed to defend himself for real. He finished his preparations with time to spare and headed into Paso Santiago an hour before Muller was to arrive.

In a town that size, which was filled with underworld figures of all sorts, finding Varillo's representative wouldn't be too hard. Especially since a man like that would be like a celebrity among a den of thieves, killers, and smugglers.

The only thing that was bothering Clint more and more was how come he still hadn't seen much of anybody else along the trail to the border. If there was an invasion only three days away, an army the size of Varillo's would surely have scouts posted or caravans running supplies across the border as his platoons settled in.

Clint wasn't much of a military strategist, but he'd been around during the War Between the States and even the small troop movements were preceded by at least some form of traffic along their routes. Surely Varillo wouldn't be displaying his scouts in full uniform, but he would at least have to send someone over the border to make sure everything was clear this close to the big attack.

At that point, Clint started thinking to his conversations with West and Muller. According to them, Varillo had been in hiding so he could gather intelligence. Supposedly, he was well informed and had men working for him on both sides of the border.

During the entire time he'd been on this mission, he had yet to see a single one of Varillo's troops. In fact, he had yet to see any wagons or riders that could even be troops in disguise. There wasn't a whole lot of places to hide in the open trail, which meant that either the troops were extremely well hidden, or they simply weren't there at all.

Clint was still thinking about this as he rode into Paso Santiago. And the more he thought about it . . . the more uneasy he felt about being in the middle of this whole, twisted mess.

THIRTY-FOUR

Clint went to the Paso Santiago Cantina just as he had arranged with Lieutenant Muller. When he got there, the only men inside the place besides the ones who worked there were sitting at a table in the back corner. One of them, a slender Mexican with a pencil-thin mustache, wore a blue jacket with a mark of rank on the shoulder.

Walking straight up to that table, Clint couldn't help but feel as though he was heading straight into a barrel of trouble.

"I hear you're the man to talk to if I want to get in touch with Colonel Varillo," Clint said, opting for the direct approach at this late hour.

The man's uniform was unlike any Clint had seen before. It didn't even resemble the standard issue worn by the regular Mexican Army. Looking away from his other two companions, the officer studied Clint for a moment before nodding his head.

"Sí. I report to the colonel," he said.

Clint was about to continue with the speech he'd rehearsed with Lieutenant Muller, but stopped himself before he got out another word. At that moment, something else came to mind that made him feel uneasy. Suddenly, his instincts screamed at him to get away from the cantina.

Get away from Paso Santiago.

Just get away before he took yet another step in the wrong direction.

"Is there . . . something you wish to say, señor?" the officer asked. The expression on his face was more expectant than confused. In fact, he didn't even look wary of the fact that he'd been picked out of a crowd so easily by a complete stranger.

"Actually," Clint said, "there is something I'd like to say." After giving each of the officer's companions a warning glance, he leaned in so that he was almost nose to nose with the officer. "I know about the spies you planted. And I know how deep your people are within the United States government."

When Clint spoke those words, he was watching for any possible reaction that they might inspire. He knew that if his gamble was a mistake, the officer would look confused or even a little aggravated at the intrusion to his conversation. But if Clint's instincts were correct, and his words struck a nerve inside the officer's mind, it would show in the other man's face.

Now, after all these years of reading men across a poker table, Clint's skills would be put to the ultimate test. And if he failed that test, it could prove disastrous for the entire country.

At first, the officer was visibly rattled. His eyes narrowed and started blinking in quick bursts, and then he started glancing nervously to the men on either side of him. "Excuse me, señor?" he asked with a vague tremor in his voice.

The signs were starting to show. Clint soaked up every detail on the officer's face as he pressed the conversation even further.

"You were expecting me, weren't you?" Clint asked.

"I . . . I don't know who—"

Clint's hand flashed to his Colt and drew the pistol before anyone at the table could even think of reacting. One moment he was speaking and in the next, he had a gun jammed beneath the officer's chin.

"You've got three seconds to answer one question," Clint snarled as a bead of perspiration worked its way out of the officer's forehead. "What's my name?"

Both of the men seated next to the officer started moving toward Clint, but before they could make it more than a few inches, the officer let out a high-pitched whine as the gun barrel was jammed up under his jaw.

"S . . . stay put," the officer moaned.

"Good idea," Clint said, thoroughly enjoying the way the other man was starting to squirm. "A man tends to get a little fidgety when he sees people closing in on him. Now what about that question? I'll give you one more second."

"I'm sure I don't—"

In a flicker of motion, Clint moved the barrel away from the officer's chin just so that could he hold the gun next to the other man's face and pull the trigger. Just as it had in his test outside of town, when the blank cartridge went off, it sounded closer to a stick of dynamite exploding inside the cantina. Everyone in the place cleared the floor at the sound and one of the men next to the officer actually fell backwards out of his seat trying to get away from the racket.

Clint's ears were ringing just as much as anyone else's, but he still kept his eyes trained on the officer. All he had to do was touch the warm, smoking barrel to the uniformed man's chin one more time to start the words flowing from his petrified mouth.

"Clint Adams," the officer sputtered. "Y . . . you're Clint Adams and you were supposed to meet me here. Clint Adams!"

"That's better," Clint said. "Now how did you know that?"

"We have . . . we have men working inside your government. They arranged this whole thing to make sure that—"

"That's quite enough," boomed a familiar voice from the front of the cantina.

Clint shoved the officer back in his seat and stepped away from the table. He immediately positioned himself with his back to a wall so he could not only keep his eye on the two men accompanying the officer but also watch the ones who'd just walked through the door.

Standing at the door, only slightly ahead of schedule, was Lieutenant Muller. In his hand was his army-issue revolver and behind him were three members of his Ghost Squadron. Muller's escorts were still dressed in their dark clothing and had remnants of camouflage paste on their skin, giving them a grayish hue.

"I was hoping you wouldn't be so smart, Adams," Muller said. "That way this could have all gone off without a hitch."

Clint held his gun at the ready, even though he knew the hammer would fall on two more blank rounds before striking live ammunition. "Sorry to disappoint you."

"That's all right. Kind of a pleasant surprise, actually. Now how about you step away from that table so we can get a nice clean shot at ya?"

THIRTY-FIVE

Clint stepped to the side as Muller had asked, placing himself in a better position to fire while making it seem as though he was simply following orders. "Did you really think I would go all the way through with your plan without stopping to ask any questions?"

"I don't know," Muller said. "You came this far without batting an eye. All you had to do was go a little further and your part would have been played out."

"The only reason I went along with any of this at all was that you managed to get the right person to vouch for you."

"Since you're gonna die anyway, I'll let you know that West didn't know a thing about what was going on. Actually, I requested to have him be assigned to my squadron to get him out of the way before he stumbled onto my little arrangement. When I got you instead, well, I was a little disappointed."

"So you didn't try to get me here at all?"

"Nope. That part was just you outsmarting yourself. Since you were happy to think I needed you so badly, I nodded and went along with it. West never told me you were so full of yourself."

147

Clint felt a pang of anger in the back of his mind. It was directed at himself more than Muller because the lieutenant had been right in his last statement. Clint had been so convinced that he was important to Muller's plan that he'd overlooked any other possibility. Whether or not that had cost him in the long run was something better left alone. Hopefully, Clint would have time to kick himself for it later.

"Just out of curiosity," Muller said. "What made you think to go against the plan now?"

Already, the man in the uniform as well as his two guards had moved away from the table to stand next to the bar. Muller and his men were inside the cantina now and spread across the front door like a firing squad, every one of their guns trained on Clint.

Lowering his Colt so that it hung at his side, Clint held the pistol so he could slowly move his thumb down toward the cylinder. "I've got to admit that I didn't suspect much of anything until last night. Having Rebecca Chase ride into camp like that wasn't the smartest thing you could've done.

"But that was just something that got me thinking. Even before I got here, you've been doing your damndest to put off any military strike against Varillo. And once I got here and started really looking around, I realized that your squadron was still a bit too far away from the border with an invasion supposedly only four days . . . make that three days away."

A crooked smile worked its way onto Muller's face. His shoulders began shaking as a low wave of laughter ran through his body. "You don't believe the invasion's coming?"

"I may not be a military genius, but common sense tells me that any army worth its salt would have to be running supplies, scouts, or even a couple of advance troops into place before storming across the border. I rode all the way here without seeing much of anything and in land like this, there sure aren't a whole lot of places for them to go.

"Also," Clint added, "your officer here was the final hole needed to sink your story. Why would a high-ranking member of an army whose very survival counts on keeping its head down low be sitting in full uniform in the middle of a cantina? Should I just assume he didn't have anything else better to do before marching in to take on the United States?"

Nodding, Muller locked eyes with Clint as the smile slowly faded away. "So tell me . . . did all of this occur to you before or after you disarmed your gun the way I asked?"

"You know something?" Clint said. "That's another thing that should have tipped me off a lot sooner. After all, it's not exactly smart to send in a vital member of your team with blank ammunition."

"You're right about that. Unless, of course, that particular member wasn't supposed to make it out of here alive."

Clint could hear his time running out as Muller's body tensed. He knew he had to keep the other man talking, if only for another minute or two while his thumb turned the cylinder of his Colt. He knew the soldiers would be watching him like hawks, so he didn't dare make any sudden moves.

"So you get me down here and get me killed," Clint said. "So what? What is that supposed to accomplish?"

"I told you, Adams. I didn't want to kill you. But since you're the one that's poking around inside my operation, that means you're the one that's got to die. It ain't nothing personal. Just business."

Besides buying himself time, Clint was beginning to see more of what Muller was doing with every word that came out of the lieutenant's mouth. "What kind of business is that? Smuggling for Varillo? Or is the colonel just a name

you used to justify everything you've been doing for the
last year or so?"

"Oh, Varillo's real enough. And so is the invasion. It
may not be coming in three days, but it's on its way. And
when it does, nobody will see it coming until it rolls right
through Washington, D.C."

Now it was Clint's turn to laugh. When he did, Muller
glared at him through angry slits and his gun hand started
trembling with rage.

"What's so damn funny?" Muller asked.

Clint's thumb moved the cylinder in his Colt one more
click, making the live ammunition next in line to fire.
"You're funny, Muller. Actually, this whole thing strikes
me as funny."

The men on either side of the lieutenant looked between
Clint and their commanding officer, unsure of what they
should do. The uniformed Mexican and his men held their
ground, waiting for Muller as well.

Clint's eyes stayed right where they had been when he'd
started laughing. At the same moment he'd gotten his Colt
ready to fire, he spotted something familiar about one of
Muller's men. All of them had been wearing their dark
clothes and black bandannas around their necks and faces.

All but one.

That one soldier waited for Clint to look his way before
pulling down his bandanna and locking eyes with him.
Rather than be surprised, Clint felt relieved as that particular soldier started bringing up his pistol and pointing it
at a different target.

Muller's voice struck through the air like cold metal.
"I've had more than my fill of you, Adams. I tried to do
this the easy way and kill you quick without you even
knowing what was coming. But if I got to take my chances
against you and possibly get me or some of my men killed
in the process, then so be it. At least I'll see you dead no
matter what."

While Clint kept up his laughter, he could tell that the attention of every man in the cantina was focused on him. That was fine by him, since it allowed that one soldier to work his way behind Muller and point his gun to the back of his head.

"If I were you," Clint said. "I'd worry about cleaning up my own backyard before worrying about invading anyone else's."

Confused, Muller paused just before pulling his trigger. "What did you say?"

But he didn't need to hear another word of Clint's explanation. Instead, the lieutenant felt the press of a gun barrel against the back of his skull, followed by the click of a hammer being pulled back.

At that moment, everyone in the cantina except for Clint, Muller, and the soldier behind him burst into motion. They scattered into positions behind tables, against the wall, or closer to the door as they suddenly realized that things had gone very, very wrong.

"How's this for a coincidence," Clint said to the soldier at Muller's back. "We were just talking about you, Rebecca."

THIRTY-SIX

Rebecca had it all down pat. Wrapping herself in layers of clothing that were bulky enough to hide her figure and give her a more blocky outline, she'd also managed to blend in with Muller's men well enough to slip in among them undetected. With her hair tied back inside one bandanna while using another to cover the lower part of her face, the rest of her disguise was taken care of by the dark camouflage worn by all of Muller's Ghost Squadron.

But the moment she'd pulled down the bandanna and looked Clint square in the eye, she'd exposed herself to someone who had a particular knack for remembering women. Although Clint wasn't sure what she would do, he was certain she'd prove to be an excellent distraction that might just be enough to pull his fat out of this fire.

Everything else up to this point had been a gamble.

So far . . . it was paying off.

"What the hell?" Muller said as he turned around to look at who had betrayed him. When he saw Rebecca in her painted face and borrowed clothes, it took him a moment to believe that he was actually looking at her. When it sank in, he clenched his teeth and started to move as though he'd forgotten about the pistol against his skull.

"If you don't think I'll kill you," Rebecca said simply, "then you aren't half as smart as I thought you were."

Muller kept himself from bringing his gun all they way up. "You're still outgunned, bitch. Back off now and I'll give you a running start. For old time's sake."

Clint knew that he wasn't going to get any better of an opening than this. So rather than let it go by, he took a deep breath and played his hand for all it was worth. "I could care less what you've got arranged with Varillo," he shouted. "The way I see it, any plan you've got falls apart without you to carry it out."

Knowing full well the hell he would unleash, Clint raised his arm and brought his gun up to fire.

Muller's head snapped around to look at Clint. "Kill 'em both!" he hollered.

And then the air exploded in a fiery hailstorm of lead.

Clint knew he would be the first target, so after taking one step forward, he launched himself to the side as the first volley of gunfire whipped through the air above his head. The blood pounded through his veins and his heart slammed like a war drum. After falling for what felt like an eternity, he finally hit the floor and rolled for the cover of a nearby table.

He could feel the impact of the soldiers' boots against the floor as they rushed toward him. Knowing that he would last another couple seconds at the most inside the cantina, he pulled his boots beneath him and spun on the balls of his feet toward the back of the room.

Even though he couldn't find what he was looking for right away, he started moving anyway. Keeping his head down and his feet moving, Clint scuttled across the floor, overturning tables and chairs to cover his wake. Every step he took brought him closer to the end of the bar. And when he finally made it there, he dove behind the wooden structure and took a quick look behind him.

The first thing he saw was a figure clad in black rushing

at him with arms outstretched. Clint acted on instinct,
dropping down and lashing out with one leg to sweep the
approaching soldier's feet out from under him. Before he
could react, the soldier was toppling sideways, his arms
flailing one way while his legs went the other.

Clint heard the soldier land with a solid *thump*, but
didn't stick around to watch. Instead, he was more concerned with pulling himself behind the bar as the rest of
Muller's men came charging toward him.

Gunshots blasted through the air, tearing chips from the
bar and punching holes in the floor that Clint had just left
behind. As he kept making his way along the bar, Clint
caught a hint of motion in the corner of his eye and spun
around to see what it was.

He twisted his body around in a tight spiral, bringing
the Colt to bear on a figure to his immediate left. When
he could see the figure head-on, Clint could see the stark
terror in the other person's eyes. The man Clint found was
a pudgy Mexican wearing a brown shirt and faded denim
pants. His face was covered with greasy stubble and his
features were contorted in a frightened mask.

"No, señor. *Por favor* . . . I'm jus' the bartender!"

Clint could hear the footsteps coming closer. Some were
following in his tracks while others were working their
way around the other side of the bar. "Is there a back
door?" Clint asked hastily.

Although the bartender was too scared to speak, he
pointed a stubby finger toward a curtain hanging on the
wall next to a shelf full of bottles. Suddenly, his eyes went
wide and his head disappeared beneath his arms as one of
the uniformed man's guards lunged over the bar and tried
to grab Clint by the back of the neck.

Twisting on his heel, Clint snatched the guard's wrist
and pulled the man over the bar using his own momentum
as well as the motion of his spin. There was a wet snapping
sound as the guard's arm broke just before he landed head-

first behind the bar. Even with the pain of his injury, the guard bared his teeth and brought his other arm around to point a gun at Clint's face.

The instant he saw the guard's pistol, Clint was a blur of motion. First, he continued his spinning motion until he was facing the curtain the bartender had shown him. As his body stopped turning, his arm kept wrapping around until the Colt was brought into position. The pistol barked once, blasting a hole through the guard's head as Clint launched himself toward the curtain.

Not bothering to see how many more soldiers were on his heels, Clint covered his face with his arms and braced his shoulders for whatever lay behind that curtain. Even if the bartender had been lying to him, Clint charged with enough force that he hoped to break through the wall if that was what he needed to do to escape the cantina.

Dull, crushing pain enveloped Clint's shoulder as he slammed against solid wood. His ears were filled with gunshots and the sound of boards cracking against his weight. After that, he toppled awkwardly through the air and then landed with a bump on dirt-covered ground.

Clint knew better than to question his good luck. Instead, he pushed aside the pain coursing through his body, got to his feet, and bolted away from the door, which he'd all but knocked off its hinges.

THIRTY-SEVEN

Muller fumed where he stood, glaring down the barrel of the gun in Rebecca's hand. If looks could kill, he wouldn't have had a thing to worry about from the pistol since the woman holding it would have been burned to cinders long before she'd been able to pull the trigger.

"I suppose the money I paid you wasn't enough," Muller said in a voice that radiated his hatred like rays from the sun. "Is that what this is all about?"

Rebecca shook her head, her eyes darting back and forth as the black-clad soldiers stormed through the cantina. "I may not have a lot of time left, so I sure as hell aren't going to explain myself to you."

"It don't matter anyway. Because your time just ran out."

With that, Rebecca saw a blur of motion out of the corner of her eye. She tried to step away from it, but she wasn't quite fast enough to avoid the Mexican guard who'd snuck up on her blind side before pouncing in for the kill.

Knowing that she was going to have to fight for her life, she tossed common sense aside and threw herself directly at the oncoming attacker. Although the Mexican was

156

slightly surprised by her choice of actions, he wasn't about to be bested by a woman nearly half his size. The burly guard angled himself to meet her head-on and swung his arm across in a wide arc when her gun arm got within his reach.

Rebecca wanted to make her one shot count, so the instant she realized that the Mexican was attempting to disarm her, she twisted her body around to the best angle possible and pulled her trigger. The gun was bigger than the ones she was used to handling and when it bucked in her hand, the recoil jerked her hand off target.

Grunting in pain, the Mexican kept coming even as a piece of his upper arm disintegrated in a red, chunky mist. The smoke from her gun stung his eyes, but he still managed to wrap his fist around Rebecca's hand, crushing her fingers against the handle of her gun.

Rebecca cried out as the bones in her hand started grinding together. As hard as she struggled to get away from the huge Mexican, it was as though she'd been anchored to her spot. When she saw his other hamlike fist coming around toward her face, she took one last shot, bringing her knee straight up into the man's groin.

She watched as the Mexican's face twisted up in pain. The swing he'd been taking stopped in mid-flight, but rather than drop him to the floor, the blow seemed to have a slightly different effect. The Mexican's eyes narrowed into angry slits and he bared his teeth like an animal.

"I gonna make you pay for that, lady," he rasped.

Lashing out with every survival instinct she had, Rebecca beat her free hand against the Mexican's side while kicking every part of him her feet could reach. But no matter where she hit him, it was as though she was fighting a brick wall. The Mexican was bringing his fist up high and cocking it all the way back, an anticipatory grin sliding onto his face.

Before the blow came at her, Rebecca could hear what

had to be Muller moving around behind her. It was then that she knew her end was near, so she closed her eyes and braced herself for whichever injury got to her first.

Rather than feel the impact of the Mexican's knuckles against her face or Muller's bullet in her back, what she felt was something pressing on the top of her head, forcing her down almost to her knees. When she was as low as she could get with her arm still in the Mexican's grasp, there was a sudden rush of air over her head and the sickening crunch of bone and cartilage caving in beneath a savage blow.

Rebecca instinctively tried to pull her arm back, but it was still held tight in the Mexican's fist. Then, there was another crunch, only this time there was a softer, slightly wetter feel to the noise that hadn't been there before.

This time, she was able to get her hand free and as soon as she realized it, she felt herself being pulled backward by something attached to her coat. When her eyes snapped open, the first thing she saw was the Mexican teetering on his heels like a bottle getting ready to fall off the fence post. His face was a twisted, blood-covered mush and there wasn't the slightest hint of consciousness in his eyes.

Still moving backward, Rebecca spotted Muller close to the bar, turning around with a surprised look on his face as though he'd forgotten she was even there. Just then, Rebecca realized that she was out the door and in front of the cantina.

As soon as she came to a stop, she wheeled around to see that Clint Adams had a hold of the collar of her coat. "What the hell are you doing?" she asked.

Clint shook his other hand while flexing his fingers, his knuckles covered in blood. "The same thing you did for me a couple minutes ago. Now let's get out of here before we're both dead!"

THIRTY-EIGHT

Clint and Rebecca were barely able to duck behind another building before Muller's soldiers came running around from the back of the cantina. Their steps pounded against the ground like a stampede, making it easy for both of them to know right when to get down behind a low wall as the soldiers walked right past them.

Keeping his head down, Clint let himself grab a seat on the ground as he reloaded his Colt with six real cartridges. As he stuffed the shells into the cylinder, he turned to Rebecca and asked, "So what was that all about?"

"I've been working with Muller for a couple months now," she said. "For most of that time I've been easing my way into Varillo's confidence and reporting back to Muller."

"Until today, I take it."

"That's right. Until today."

"So what convinced you to jump sides?"

Stepping to the corner of the building, Rebecca took a quick look around the corner. When she didn't catch sight of any of their pursuers, she went back to Clint's side and sat down. "Nothing had to convince me. I was never really on his side to begin with."

Clint eyed her suspiciously as he flicked the Colt closed. "You're a spy for Varillo?"

"No," she said with a tired smile. "But you're getting warmer." Giving Clint a moment to stew, she rubbed her face with her hands and wiped away some of the crusted camouflage. "I work for the United States government. You're better acquainted with a colleague of mine by the name of Jeremy West."

The suspicion on Clint's face darkened even further as he tightened his grip on the Colt. "Why didn't he ever mention you?"

"Because of what I just told you. I'm playing both sides here and if either one of them found out, I'd have been shot on sight. He knew that better than anybody."

"So how do I know I can trust you? After all, you might just be trying to get in good with me."

"There are much easier ways to do that. Besides, you heard it straight from the source. Muller and Varillo are working together and they don't have much further to go before they're ready to move. I've been able to sneak my way into a couple patrols here and there, but I haven't gotten into anything that's too heavily guarded. You, on the other hand, might have gotten to see some things I couldn't. It's a man's world, after all."

Clint studied Rebecca closely, thinking back to all the times he'd seen her before. "So what were you doing in Labyrinth?" he asked.

"I was assigned to stick close to Gerard Lantiss, one of Varillo's men. I discovered that one of Muller's men was there on Varillo's behalf, but didn't know for sure until he broke Lantiss out of jail. I don't know how he did it, but I never saw Simmons once."

"Simmons was the name of the guy Muller sent?"

"That's right. My sources told me he'd be there, but he did a good job of hiding himself, because all I found was the deputy he killed while breaking Lantiss free."

"So what have you found out after working this long as a spy in both camps?" Clint asked.

"Most of the information I got was from Varillo. He's collecting troops and weapons, preparing for a major offensive, but that's old news by now. I've made reports back to Washington about where some of his bases are located, but I'm sure I don't know all of them.

"Varillo is well armed and has plenty of men. In fact, he could have a real chance of taking over the Mexican government. But he's obsessed with an invasion. All he talks about is riding into America because his own country isn't enough of a challenge.

"Sometimes after we . . ." Glancing at Clint, she suddenly turned her head away as though she was embarrassed. ". . . sometimes he brags to me about how he'll take control of Mexico after he's carved out a piece of America for himself." She raised her head again, a fresh strength showing in her features. "As far as I could tell, the only thing holding him back was a way to get into this country. He may be crazy, but he's not stupid enough to just form ranks and march over the border."

"Did you ever see the tunnels?" Clint asked.

"Tunnels? I don't think so."

"Believe me, you'd know them if you saw them. They're a system of mines that have been built into a network of tunnels beneath Perro Rojo. Muller took me down there once. I'm not sure if he meant to as some kind of test or if it was just circumstances, but he told me they're being expanded all the way down to the border."

Rebecca snapped her fingers as a look of realization lit up her face. "I remember hearing something about that, but I've never actually seen them. They're supposed to be used more for transporting troops and supplies."

"Yeah, well, that's exactly what Muller's been using them for. I didn't see more than a mile or so of them, but they could stretch on for a hell of a lot more than that."

"And now that we know for sure that Muller's gone bad . . ."

"You mean you didn't know that already?" Clint asked.

"I told you, he kept me at arm's length. Most of the contacts I have are among his men. Some have their suspicions, but others say he's the best commander since Grant."

"Now it's plain enough why you heard such conflicting reports."

Nodding, Rebecca said, "Not all of the Ghost Squadron are in on this with him. I knew there were at least a few good men in his outfit. That's how I got a hold of these," she said while tugging at the clothing she wore. "That's why Muller was able to keep me guessing for so long. I mean, if he could lie to his own men so convincingly, it wouldn't be too hard to string me along. But we've got just about the entire picture now."

"Muller and the men he's taken into his confidence are working with Varillo, probably arranging to bring in his troops using the system of tunnels. And once Varillo has access to that, he's got free reign to come and go as he pleases."

"He could bring in assassins or terrorist squads, do his damage, and then get away scot-free with Muller smuggling him underground. Hell," Rebecca said with a faraway look in her eyes, "the Ghost Squadron might even be the ones assigned to go after Varillo, giving both him and Muller that much power. Once anyone found out about it . . ."

"It would be too late," Clint finished.

The soldiers' voices were getting closer. Clint could sense them closing in on their position like impending doom.

"Well, none of that's going to happen," he said. "Now that we know about what's going on, we can put a stop to it before it goes any further."

Rebecca felt the same anxiousness as Clint. She glanced nervously around the corner and immediately pulled her head back. "There's two of them coming this way," she whispered. "I can help you, but first I need to get a gun. That big bastard kept a hold of mine."

"Getting a gun won't be a problem," Clint said. "When you get it, just be sure you're ready to use it. We came in on this at the last minute and if we have to come back for Muller, we won't have half as good a chance as we've got right now."

Suddenly, Rebecca leaned forward and planted a kiss on Clint's lips. The tension running through both of their bodies lent even more fire to their sudden embrace. When she pulled back, Rebecca said, "That was to thank you for saving my life."

Clint gave her a quick smile. "Don't worry. I haven't forgotten about what you did for me as well. I'll show you my thanks when we have a bit more time. You just stay put and I'll fetch you a pistol."

THIRTY-NINE

The soldier knew his prey had to be close by. He could smell their fear like a sweet scent leading him directly to its source. His hand closed around the grip of his pistol as he circled around a small dry goods store across from the cantina. After checking out the other buildings in the immediate vicinity, he knew this had to be the one.

Since he'd gotten left behind in the initial scuffle inside the cantina, the soldier was itching to get his hands dirty in this fight. That, as well as the reward he would surely get from Lieutenant Muller, inspired him to move even faster down the alleyway toward the only place the two runaways could be hiding.

The great Clint Adams, he thought as he moved. What a joke.

Approaching the rear of the building, the soldier pressed himself up against the wall and took one more step toward the corner. He could hear voices now, talking in hushed tones less than twenty feet away.

One more step . . .

The next thing the soldier saw was something rushing toward his face so quickly that it was only a blur in motion. As soon as he saw it, the thing slammed into his face, knocking his head back into the wall with a sickening thud.

After that, everything around him started to teeter back and forth. The world spun faster and faster until there wasn't anything around him but approaching darkness.

Suddenly he was on the ground . . .

. . . getting tired . . .

Clint stepped around the corner, the board he'd used to cave in the soldier's face still gripped in both hands. Approaching the dark figure carefully, he prepared himself to hit the other man again, but soon realized that wouldn't be necessary. The man's eyes were open, but there was nobody home.

Just to be sure, Clint nudged the soldier with the toe of his boot before he was satisfied that the man was down for good. The first thing he did was pluck the gun from the sleeping man's hand.

"Here," Clint whispered as Rebecca stepped around the corner. "Take this." He tossed the gun into her waiting hand, tensing himself just in case he'd been wrong about her the entire time.

But Rebecca didn't do anything besides check the pistol over and make sure the cylinder was full before walking to Clint's side. "Do you want to go after Muller, or should I?" she asked.

"All I want you to do is find that one dressed in the military uniform."

"You mean the Mexican who was in the cantina?"

"That's the one. Do you know if he was for real?"

Rebecca shrugged. "I don't recognize his face, but the clothes he wore were similar to the uniform worn by Varillo's men."

"That's good enough for now. Go after that one and make sure he doesn't get away. I'll take care of Muller and the rest of the men he brought with him. If you hear shooting, just keep your head down and wait for me."

"But how will I know if . . ."

"Bring the Mexican back to this spot and wait for me. If I don't find you in an hour, then get all the information out of him as you can and get the hell out of here. Try to stay alive until you can report back to Washington."

"Clint, I . . ." Rebecca stopped herself before saying anything else. She knew there were things she wanted to tell him, despite the fact that she'd only met him one other time before this day. Before she could think about it any further, she felt Clint's arm wrap around her and pull her up against him.

Once again, his lips pressed against hers. Only this time, they allowed themselves to explore each other a bit more. Rebecca let her tongue slip into Clint's mouth so she could taste him while letting herself melt into his arms. She reached up to slide her hand along the back of his neck before running her fingers through his hair.

Although they kissed for only a few seconds, it was long enough to take them away from Paso Santiago. While their tongues mingled and their hands roamed, they didn't allow themselves to think about the killing they'd seen or the danger that lay ahead.

All they thought about was each other.

And then . . . just as suddenly as it had started . . . it was over.

They eased apart from each other, reluctant to end the pleasant distraction even though they knew they had more important business that needed their attention. For a few more seconds, they simply looked into the other's eyes.

"We'll finish this later," Rebecca said. And then, hopefully, she added, "Won't we?"

Clint brushed the dark hair away from her face and nodded. "Oh, you can count on it. Just make sure to keep yourself in one piece so I can make good on that."

"Good luck, Clint."

Nodding, Clint expressed his thoughts by allowing his

hand to linger against her skin for another second. When he turned away from her, he listened for the biggest source of noise in the area. By the sound of it, Muller's men and some more of the Mexican officer's guards had joined forces. Clint only hoped that that meant the officer himself would be an easy target for Rebecca.

He took one more look over his shoulder and found that Rebecca had already disappeared. Doing his best to put everything else out of his mind, he knelt down to the fallen soldier's body and started pulling off the man's coat and bandanna.

As Clint worked, he could hear Muller's men getting closer. They knew he was there. They might have even heard the scuffle that had dropped their comrade. And now, they were circling in like vultures who could already taste the carrion in their throats.

Clint finished up what he was doing and ran away from the body. It was time to do some circling of his own.

FORTY

Muller could feel the hairs standing up on the back of his neck. His flesh was crawling as though it wanted to pull away from his bones, and every muscle in his body was trembling. Standing in front of the cantina, he glared at the only one of his men who was still in eyeshot and had to fight back the urge to take a swing at the man.

"Where the fuck is Captain Benito?" Muller asked.

The soldier looked around as though he expected to see the Mexican officer hiding beneath a nearby rock. "He skipped out when the fight started. I guess he probably went—"

Wheeling around on the soldier with his pistol gripped beneath white knuckles, Muller snarled, "I don't want to hear about your guesses! Either you know where he is, or you don't!"

"Then I don't know, sir."

"Find him. If Adams is the one that was sent in West's place, then he'll be after more than a way out of town. More than likely, he'll want to either get his hands on me or the captain."

"Shouldn't someone stay here, then, in case he comes after you first?"

"Don't worry about me," Muller hissed. "If he comes after me, then all our problems will be solved. He'll go after that Mexican first, I'll bet. Benito's the easiest target and that's the one that all them gunfighter types would go after.

"I've seen enough of them with Varillo to know they ain't got the salt to take on someone who might actually be a match for them. Didn't you see how he ran out of that cantina? He may be the Gunsmith, but that don't make him any more of a man."

The soldier nodded and gave a crisp salute. Although the gesture looked somewhat out of place coming from someone dressed more like a bandit, it was given in a precise manner and was given with every bit of respect the soldier could show. When the lieutenant returned his salute, the soldier rushed off to go about his duty. The moment he was away from Muller, he became just another shadow in the desolate streets.

Muller looked around him with his hands clasped behind his back. The only sign he got that the town wasn't deserted was the occasional tentative face peeking out from behind a drawn window shade or a door held slightly ajar, only to be slammed shut when Muller turned his eyes that way.

Even though he couldn't see them, Muller knew his men were out there. They were the best at what they did. He knew that because he'd been the one to train them.

He'd taught them how to stalk.

How to hunt.

He'd taught them how to shoot.

How to kill.

The more he thought about the hunt that was going on all around him, the more Muller wanted to be a part of it himself. He knew it was his place as commander to watch the progress of battle and advise which way it should turn at any given time, but he felt as though he'd be missing out on a truly magnificent experience.

To hunt down someone like Clint Adams. Cowardly gunfighter or not, the man was still a legend and killing him would be a victory that only one man in the world could ever claim.

It wouldn't be hard . . . especially with his men out there to flush Adams out from wherever he was hiding. And when it came time to put a bullet between the Gunsmith's eyes, there was no reason it couldn't be Muller himself who pulled the trigger.

The lieutenant closed his eyes and leaned his head back, taking in a deep breath of battlefield air. That was the sweetest thing any soldier could smell. And no matter how many times he'd pulled the acrid mixture of fear, gunpowder and adrenaline into his lungs, he would never get tired of it.

Slowly, Muller turned and walked to where he knew his men were concentrating their search. Paso Santiago wasn't a large town and he'd been there enough times to know it like the back of his hand. There were only so many places to hide and Muller knew his men were intimately familiar with them all.

As he stalked through the streets and alleyways, every one of his senses were working at their peak performance. At times, he swore he could smell a hint of Rebecca's skin.

He would deal with her later.

His hand clenched around his pistol, thumb pulling back the hammer in anticipation.

Battlefield air . . . there was nothing sweeter.

FORTY-ONE

Clint had been the prey almost as many times as he'd been the hunter. In fact, living as a man who was known by every punk with a gun trying to make a name for himself, he lived every day of his life as someone's prey. The only difference was that he wasn't exactly the easiest prey to kill.

Over the years, his instincts had been sharpened to a razor's edge, steering him toward the most likely places where the hunters were and letting him know which sounds he heard were harmless and which needed to be feared. Walking from building to building, Clint might have been mistaken for a sleepwalker. His steps were slow and sure, taking him into doorways, stopping, and then walking on as though receiving his orders from somewhere outside of himself.

Maneuvering this way, he barely made a sound as he opened the door of the next building he came to and stepped inside. He found himself inside a small home, knowing that a glare from him would be enough to send the two elderly residents retreating for one of the other rooms. Sure enough, the pair shuffled away from him al-

most immediately, their footsteps soon cut off by the sound
of a door slamming upstairs.

Clint peeked outside through the window and quickly
went about his preparations.

The soldier knew he'd seen Adams heading this way only
a minute or two ago. After tailing the other man down the
adjacent alley, the only other place he could have gone
was across the street. Since he couldn't see so much as a
hint of motion in the street or anywhere near it, the black-
clad figure turned toward the little two-level house and
snapped the hammer back on his pistol.

He could hear something moving about inside the house.
It wasn't the panicked steps of any local, either, but the
careful motions of someone trying to lay low and not be
seen. The soldier made his way to a small window next to
the house's back door. Taking a quick look through the
glass, he spotted the face that he'd last seen in Paso Santiago's cantina.

Not wanting to take any chances with Adams, he
jumped onto the landing and bashed open the door with
one swift kick. He found himself looking directly into the
face of Clint Adams, a feeling of pure victory washing
through his body.

"Adios, asshole," the soldier sneered as he squeezed his
trigger, pulled back the hammer and fired again.

The first shot put a hole right in the middle of Adams's
face. The next shattered his head all the way down past
his neck until there was nothing left put a blank wooden
board.

Staring at the spot Adams had been, the soldier took
another step inside the house. His jaw hung open in utter
confusion . . . until his boots crunched against the broken
glass on the floor.

By then it was too late.

Spinning around, in response to the sound of a single

footstep, the soldier was just in time to look down the barrel of Adams's gun before he heard the deafening roar of the Colt.

Clint watched the soldier drop, the other man's brains leaking out from the fresh hole in his skull. Then, he turned to look at the broken remains of the mirror he'd propped up in front of the door at just enough of an angle to reflect his own image toward the doorway.

After tossing a couple of dollars onto the floor amid the glass to cover the damages, Clint bent down, took what he needed from the soldier, and moved on.

Corporal Peters had been taught by the best. He tracked Adams through the streets of Paso Santiago like a rabbit through the woods behind his ranch back home. Lieutenant Muller had taught him that hunting men and animals wasn't all that different. Both did anything they could to survive, but one was a much more satisfying kill to make.

Even though Peters hadn't been on Adams's trail since the hunt began like the rest of the men, he was confident that he could pick up the scent easily enough. The streets were as still as a photograph and almost just as silent.

There had been the occasional sound of a struggle, but Peters knew better than to jump at every little thing he heard. Especially when the target was as good as Adams was supposed to be.

It wasn't until he heard the sound of a gunshot coming from down the street that Peters allowed his hopes to rise. Making sure to keep his head down and his body in the shadows, Peters hustled toward the spot the noise had come from and slowed to a halt when he detected something else moving in the alley ahead.

Holding his pistol at the ready, he expertly stepped around anything that would alert the person ahead of him. His feet narrowly avoided disturbing even the smallest bit of paper until he was less than ten feet away from a figure crouched in shadow.

"Stay right there," he said while sighting down his barrel. "On your feet and turn around."

The figure did as Peters commanded, straightening up to reveal the black coat hanging over his frame as well as the dark grime on his hands. When he turned around, the bottom part of his face was covered with a black bandanna.

"Jesus," Peters said as he lowered his gun. "You nearly got yourself killed."

"Yeah," Clint said as he tugged the bandanna down. "That would've been unfortunate."

Peters reacted with reflexes that had been honed over years of close-quarters combat.

But Clint's had been formed over a lifetime and he managed to clear leather and fire before the other man could even lift his arm.

FORTY-TWO

Lieutenant Muller heard the gunshots and he knew that his men had found Clint Adams. Although he would have liked to think that he'd trained the soldiers well enough to put a bullet through Adams's head before the gunfighter could get a shot off, he knew the Gunsmith's reputation had to stand for something.

At least one of his men was probably dead. And however many Adams had hurt, that was how many holes Muller figured on putting through Adams's brain.

He walked straight toward the building where the most recent shot had come from. Focusing his eyes on what was directly in front of him, Muller tensed his body for the final fight, hoping that his men had left him a piece of Adams before hurting him too bad.

Something in the back of his mind told him that Adams wasn't dead, however. It was that same combat sense that let him know whenever he had to worry about an ambush or be on the lookout for snipers. And it was that same inner sense that told him not to charge around the next corner without preparing himself for what could be waiting for him on the other side.

Pausing before he walked around the building, Muller

lowered his head and made a quick leap into the alley, raising his gun and tensing his finger upon the trigger. But there wasn't anything in that alley besides piles of collected trash and a few empty crates.

Muller walked down the alley without making a sound. The wind made more noise than he did as it brushed along the sides of the buildings to his left and right, dusting the ground like a gentle hand brushing back a baby's hair.

Finally, Muller stepped out of the alley and into a large courtyard shared by both buildings. The moment he walked into the open, he knew there was somebody else in that courtyard. Somebody was waiting for him, and Muller was more than ready. His hand twitched around his weapon when he saw the figure standing before him.

The man just stood there with his hands at his sides, the edges of his brown duster flapping idly in the breeze.

"What's the matter, Adams?" Muller asked. "You get tired of running?"

Clint lifted his head slowly, his eyes appearing beneath the rim of his hat like two inverted sunrises. His voice was the same pitch as thunder brewing in the distance. "You could say that," he replied.

Muller eyed him across the thirty feet or so that separated them. A wry smirk crawled onto his face and he lifted his face to the wind. "All right, boys," he called out. "Let's show this gunfighter how we handle our problems."

As the seconds ticked by, the only thing that even made an attempt to answer him was the wind itself. Clint stood and watched the lieutenant with growing interest. He particularly enjoyed the way the smile on Muller's face kept growing, as though he truly thought he had every possible angle worked out.

Finally, Clint reached into his pocket. He saw the way Muller's hand twitched on his weapon, so he only used three fingers to slowly pull out a clump of material and hold it out for the other man to see. Once he saw Muller ease off his pistol, Clint tossed the contents of his pocket onto the ground between himself and Muller.

All three black bandannas from each one of Muller's soldiers dropped to the dirt. They lay there as the wind blew around them, causing the edges of the scarves to twitch as though imitating the last convulsions before death.

Muller stared down at the bandannas and then back up to Clint. He looked back and forth again and again, each time his face becoming redder, his eyes wider.

". . . No . . ." Muller whispered. "This can't be. I trained those men. They were . . . they were the best."

"You might have trained them," Clint said in a voice that was carried by the wind to assault Muller's ears. "But you should never have thought they were the best. You see . . . that spot's already taken."

Clint's words had the exact effect he'd been looking for.

When he heard them, Muller staggered back a step as every bit of color drained out of his face. His hands started trembling at his sides and when he lifted his gun to take a shot at Clint, he squeezed his trigger in a panic and sent his first round into the ground several feet off target.

Taking his time, Clint lifted his arm and sighted down his barrel. He didn't even flinch as Muller took another shot, this time sending a bullet whipping through the air to Clint's right side.

Just then, a realization settled upon Lieutenant Muller. It was the last, terrifying revelation that filled every hunter's mind just before they were sent to their maker. He knew he was beaten. And as that simple notion became a reality, he let out a primal howl, his finger clenching on the trigger one more time.

But Clint wasn't about to stand there for shot number three. Instead, he fired the Colt once into Muller's shoulder to pull his gun arm off center. The next round cut through the air and drilled a neat hole through Muller's skull, spinning the lieutenant around on the ball of one foot and dropping him facefirst onto the pile of black bandannas.

Clint spun the pistol once around his finger and dropped it back into its holster. He nearly drew it again when he heard footsteps rushing toward him from the alley behind him. Turning around with his hand poised over his holster, Clint relaxed as soon as he saw who was approaching.

"It's only me," Rebecca said as she slowed to a walk. Her breath was coming in quick gasps and her face was red with exhaustion. "I see you found Muller without much problem. Are you hurt?"

"I'm not sure if I should call it easy, but I managed. What about Varillo's officer? Did you catch up with him?"

Rebecca shook her head. "I caught sight of him getting onto his horse, but there were at least half a dozen other guards with him. I got a few of them, but all they wanted to do was make sure Captain Benito got away. I'm sorry."

It felt as though it had been forever since Clint had smiled, but he broke that dry spell when he walked up to Rebecca and put his hand on her shoulder. "No need for apologies. Let him run all he wants. We know where to catch up with him. Until then, we need to get some rest. Also, I was hoping you could get your hands on some supplies so we can finish this job off right."

Rebecca slid her arm around Clint's waist. "There's a nicer town about ten miles west of here. I've kind of been using that as my safe haven during this assignment. We can lick our wounds and I can wire Washington."

"Sounds great. Although," Clint added as he patted himself down, "I think I actually managed to make it through this one without picking up any wounds along the way."

Leaning in to kiss him gently on the neck, Rebecca whispered, "Fine. Then maybe I can find something else to lick."

FORTY-THREE

The name of Rebecca's safe haven was Vista Blanca. When Clint rode into town with Rebecca on the saddle behind him, he didn't care much about the name of the place or anything else besides where the hotel was and when he could get himself into a bath. After spending the last several days tramping through mine shafts and sleeping on the ground, his nose was starting to hate the rest of his body.

After checking into a clean hotel, Clint and Rebecca shared a large, claw-foot tub, taking their time cleaning each other off and then wrapping themselves in a luxurious cotton towel. Their skin hadn't even had a chance to dry before they were under the sheet of their bed, doing their best to work up an appetite before dinner.

Clint started off at Rebecca's toes, rubbing each one in turn as she moaned silently in appreciation. He moved up past her ankles, massaging her calves and then easing his hands up over her thighs. Once he was there, he started planting little kisses on the skin that was still warm from his touch. His lips stayed near her hips while his hands crept over her stomach and then up to cup her soft, voluptuous breasts.

Running her fingers through Clint's hair, Rebecca squirmed on the mattress as his lips grazed the soft hair between her legs, his tongue reaching out to taste the soft, moist skin underneath. Closing her eyes, she held Clint in place while opening her legs and sliding her hips forward.

Unable to wait any longer, Clint opened his mouth and thrust his tongue inside of her for just a second before pulling back and doing it again. She tasted sweet and every time his lips grazed the sensitive nub of her clit, Rebecca cried out and writhed furiously beneath him.

With her juices still on his lips, Clint crawled on top of her until his hard cock was pressing between her legs. The moment he leaned down, Rebecca lifted her head to meet his lips with hers. Her muscles tensed and her arms wrapped tightly around him as Clint thrust his hips forward, driving his cock deep inside of her.

With one leg wrapped loosely around his waist while grinding her hips in time to his movements, Rebecca started to moan as the feeling of Clint moving inside of her drove her to the brink of ecstasy.

Clint looked down at her sweating body and felt his cock grow even harder. Her stomach rose and fell with each strained breath and her nipples grew stiff as he leaned down to suck them between his lips. He only stopped moving for a second and Rebecca took over, thrusting her hips up and moving herself around him, squeezing his shaft with the muscles between her legs.

The sensation was enough for both of them to climax as wave after wave of pleasure tore through their bodies. Finally, when he thought he didn't even have enough strength to hold himself up, Clint lay down on the bed next to her and let out an exhausted breath.

"That was," he said. "That was just—"

Suddenly, the door to their room burst open, causing Clint to sit bolt upright and Rebecca to instinctively roll

to the side. Even as the door slammed against the wall, the
man who'd kicked it in was already inside, his hand
wrapped around a pearl-handled .38.

"I knew you'd come here, you little bitch," Gerard Lantiss said with a victorious grin. "And bringing Adams, too?
Well, that's all the better."

Clint's eyes flashed from the gun being pointed at him
and his own Colt, which was hanging from the back of a
chair near the foot of the bed. Reaching behind him, he
was relieved when he didn't feel Rebecca on the bed.

"What do you want?" Clint asked in an attempt to buy
some time.

"Muller told me to meet him at Paso Santiago and when
I got there, he was already dead, Captain Benito was gone,
and Rebecca was riding off with you! Well, there's only
one thing to do with traitors," Lantiss said as he snapped
the .38's hammer back. "And you, Adams, are gonna make
me famous."

As a last-ditch effort, Clint threw himself toward the
foot of the bed, hoping to get to his gun belt before feeling
a bullet drill through his back. His hands were empty when
the first shot cracked through the air.

Reflexively, Clint rolled off the bed and landed on the
floor as another shot sounded.

He got a hold of his Colt and looked up to fire, but
Lantiss was no longer standing there. Clint checked him-
self over and didn't find so much as a scratch on him.
Confused, he got to his feet and checked on Rebecca.

She was kneeling on the other side of the bed, smoking
army-issue revolver in hand. Lantiss was sprawled on his
back in the hall.

"I'll be damned," Clint said.

Rebecca stood up and lowered her gun. "You might
have been if I wasn't accustomed to keeping my guns
where I could reach them. I don't know about this clunky

thing," she added while hefting the gun she'd taken from one of Muller's men. "It slowed me down a bit."

Clint shook his head and let out the breath he'd been holding.

·

FORTY-FOUR

Captain Benito was tired. In fact, after running for two days straight without more than an hour of sleep, the word *tired* barely managed to cover what he was feeling. But he kept running anyway.

Even after meeting up with a fresh contingent of seven personal guards, he kept running for the safest route he could think of to get out of the country and back to his homeland of Mexico. With images of the bloodbath he'd witnessed at Paso Santiago still fresh in his mind, he was set to personally request Colonel Varillo to step up his plans for moving into America.

Benito and his men had been moving through the underground passages all day. There was still a long way to go, but ever since he'd moved into the safety of the secret tunnels, his spirits had been improving steadily.

The few gringos he saw in the passages were on Varillo's payroll, and he let them pass without more than a casual wave. And so Benito pushed south underground, planning the report he would give to Varillo in his mind with every step he took.

In fact, he could already see Varillo's forces moving north through these tunnels clearly in his mind's eye. He could see them walking right in beneath the American's noses, ready to kill the gringos' politicians, undermine their armies, and eventually assassinate their president.

What he didn't see, however, were the crates lined up along the walls of the tunnel at their feet.

In the thick, murky blackness that filled every inch of the tunnels, the fact that Benito or any of his men simply walked over those crates was no surprise. What was even harder to see were the wires running from the crates, up into a small access tunnel that led to the surface, and ended in a small brown box topped by a simple lever.

Clint and Rebecca stood beside that box with a crew of ten men behind them.

"Your people sure work fast," Clint said to Rebecca. "You only sent the telegram to Washington two days ago and not only did those supplies I asked for get here, but your people set them all up."

Rebecca looked at the men behind her with satisfaction and then nodded to Clint. "I figure you've seen too many of the bad apples that work for the government. Now it's time to see what we can do when we put our mind to a good cause."

"Well, I can't think of a better way to celebrate my official retirement from government service," Clint said with a smile. "And like a man I once knew told me . . . if you've got to pull out, you might as well do as much damage as you can as you go."

Clint reached down, pulled the lever, and listened with satisfaction as the ground rumbled beneath his feet and the muffled sounds of hundreds of pounds of dynamite brought tons of rock and soil down to fill the tunnels leading into Mexico.

Grinning down at Rebecca, Clint said, "Now *that's* what I call a barbed arrow."

Watch for

DEAD MAN'S EYES

246th novel in the exciting GUNSMITH series
from Jove

Coming in June!